SAMANTHA
GETS BRAVE

BY MELANIE MCCLAY

ISBN-13: 978-1-7354819-1-3

Library of Congress Control Number:
2020916033

Cover design by: Milan
Printed in the United States of America

Publisher's Cataloging-In-Publication Data
(Prepared by The Donohue Group, Inc.)

Names: McClay, Melanie, author.
Title: Samantha gets brave / by Melanie McClay.
Description: [Green Valley, Arizona] : [Melanie McClay],
    [2020] | Series: [Brave Samantha series] ; [1] | Interest
    age level: 009-012. | Summary: "Samantha Taylor is
    afraid of everything ... When a brave decision leads
    Samantha into the forest, she dives into an adventurous
    treasure hunt. With dangers all around, Samantha and
    her new-found friends search for the Saez treasure
    while overcoming fears and following the clues no one
    has been able to solve for more than 150 years"--
    Provided by publisher.
Identifiers: ISBN 9781735481913 | ISBN 9781735481906
    (ebook)
Subjects: LCSH: Courage--Juvenile fiction. | Treasure
    troves--Juvenile fiction. | Wolves--Wounds and injuries--
    Juvenile fiction. | Friendship--Juvenile fiction. | CYAC:
    Courage--Fiction. | Buried treasure--Fiction. | Wolves--
    Wounds and injuries--Fiction. | Friendship--Fiction. |
    LCGFT: Detective and mystery fiction. | Action and
    adventure fiction.
Classification: LCC PZ7.1.M42213 Sa 2020 (print) | LCC
    PZ7.1.M42213 (ebook) | DDC [Fic]--dc23

To my husband, my family, and the rest of my team for your support, imagination, and attention to detail.

1

. . . .

"Let's have a sleepover at Samantha's tonight!" said Ashley.

Samantha almost choked on her peanut butter sandwich and looked at Ashley with eyebrows raised in surprise. She started coughing. Samantha was planning to read at her fort in the woods this weekend, not host a sleepover. She liked her friends, but her weekends were reserved for peaceful, quiet activities like reading and studying and more reading.

Samantha Taylor was the third-born child in a family with five rambunctious children. She wasn't exactly small for her age, but she wasn't growing as quickly as the rest of the kids in her class. Her slight frame was often covered in clothes that didn't quite fit. It looked like she was trying to hide inside the fabric. Her brown hair was a slightly lighter shade than her dark brown eyes, which rarely made eye contact with those around her. Sometimes her demeanor suggested she wanted to be invisible.

At home, Samantha often felt invisible. Her energetic family of seven kept the house filled with happiness, drama, and a lot of noise. On the weekends, Samantha would sneak out the back door and make her way to the fort she had built in the woods. It was her quiet sanctuary, and she liked to indulge herself with hours of peaceful reading time in the forest. While Samantha loved the woods and was overly familiar with the short path to her fort, she had a healthy respect for potential dangers in the forest. She never strayed far from the path, she never went past her fort, and she always headed home well before dusk. Even if the book she was reading consumed her attention, her cautious nature led her home by dinner time.

Sometimes Samantha wished she was less of a chicken and could explore beyond her fort. There could be some exciting adventures out there waiting for her. But as with so many other things in her life, she just wasn't brave enough yet.

Samantha suspected Ashley and the other girls mainly wanted the sleepover to be at her house so they could flirt with her older brother, Jack. She felt bad for thinking it, but sometimes she wondered if they would still be her friends if Jack wasn't her older brother.

Jack was the quarterback on the eighth-grade football team and all the boy-crazy girls in seventh grade knew it. Not that anyone could forget—Jack never left the house without his football in tow. He claimed that carrying the football nonstop was necessary to perform at an optimum level, but Samantha suspected he was using it to initiate conversations about football whenever he could. Samantha used to be close to her brother Jack, but since he'd joined the football team, he rarely had time for her anymore.

Ashley, Kayla, and Emma—Samantha's friends—were very aware of Jack's social status as an eighth-grade athlete and were eager to present themselves as dating options. Dating an eighth grader would certainly increase their fame in middle school and solidify their popularity.

What had happened to her friends this year? Last year, none of them had cared about boys or makeup or being popular. She could still remember them all playing with Barbies for heaven's sake. And now this year, boys were all they could talk about. "Boy crazy" was a fitting term for them now.

It was as if the summer between sixth and seventh grade had changed the three of them simultaneously. They started showing up to school in skirts and fitted tops that showed off their legs and sometimes their midriffs. Samantha hadn't changed much over the summer. And Samantha didn't feel comfortable in the kinds of clothes they wore, but she didn't want to be left out either. She was afraid of going through the seventh grade alone. Her sister, Diana, the oldest of the five kids in her family, had stepped in to help and outfitted Samantha with her one-size-too-big, but fashionable hand-me-downs. They covered all the important parts of Samantha's shorter and slimmer frame.

Ashley and the other girls had also started wearing makeup and doing their hair in more grown-up styles. Samantha couldn't stand mascara on her eyelashes—it just felt too gooey. She had settled for lip gloss and that seemed to be a good enough show of effort to solidify her position in the pretty girl clique. That and the fact Jack was her older brother.

Samantha took a sip of water and managed to stop coughing. "Maybe next weekend," she said. "I think Jack is going to a party tonight."

"A party?" Ashley squealed. "At whose house?"

"I'm not sure," Samantha said. "I think it's one of the other football players."

"It must be Matt's party," said Kayla in a hushed and very serious tone as if she were reporting an international news scandal. "I heard his parents were out of town."

The girls rambled on excitedly, talking about whether or not they might be able to get into an eighth-grade party. They gossiped about who might be there, how they were going to sneak out of their respective houses, and what they were going to wear. They went on and on about the party until Kayla mentioned her new lip gloss, and then Petunia Pink became the star of the show.

The table they were sitting at was big enough for eight people, but it was occupied by just the four of them. It was always just the four of them—no one else was ever invited to join. Kayla and Emma felt incredibly honored to be allowed to sit with Ashley at lunch, and they would never dare sit with any other groups. Samantha was just too scared to try sitting with any of the other cliques.

One day, earlier in the school year, Samantha tried to sit with a different group. Ashley had stood over Samantha until she reluctantly moved back to Ashley's table. Samantha never tried to sit with anyone else again.

Samantha sat quietly and chewed her food thoughtfully. *Is this what all girls become? Am I destined to start competing for male attention and trying to get into parties? Is this what real friendships are made of—gossiping and giggling?* She was thankful when the bell finally rang and they all headed in to their Friday afternoon classes.

As the throng of students proceeded down the hallway, one of the girls from a younger grade was bumped so hard her books fell to the ground. Loose papers were knocked free and shuffled under the feet of oblivious middle schoolers. Ashley, Kayla, and Emma pointed and giggled, but Samantha remembered what it was like to be a small sixth grader in a busy hallway. A similar incident had happened to her last year. Samantha stopped and started gathering the papers for the younger, smaller girl. By the time they picked everything up, the hallway was practically empty. The shy sixth grader said, "Thank you."

Samantha smiled in response, and then they both had to run to their respective classes to arrive before the tardy bell rang.

In social studies class they were focused on the history of their state, Arizona, and they were learning about the Apache tribes who would occasionally travel through the state. Mr. Turner, the teacher, taught them about a train robbery. The robbers stole a lot of gold and then a renegade Apache tribe set out to attack the train robbers. The Native Americans wanted the gold for themselves. When the robbers saw the Apache galloping toward them with weapons raised, they quickly dug a hole and buried their recently stolen loot by the side of the road. To this day the gold has never been found.

That was one of the reasons Mr. Turner was such a great teacher—he kept things interesting! Mr. Turner himself was an interesting man. As far as Samantha knew, he didn't have a family. The rumor was that his ex-wife used to be a Russian spy or something. Samantha was pretty sure the stories were made up, but she was curious about Mr. Turner anyway. She was just too afraid to ask him directly.

Mr. Turner told another story about lost gold in Arizona, and then he moved on to talk about the daily lives of the Navajo tribes. The Navajo were more peaceful than the Apache and lived off the land using sustainable hunting practices.

The Navajo apparently used to eat or utilize every part of a buffalo's body when they killed it. The Spanish and English settlers would kill the buffalo only for their hides. That was appallingly wasteful to the Native Americans, and Mr. Turner thought it was wasteful as well. He was passionate about animals—it was a trait Samantha admired about him.

Last summer, volunteering at the animal shelter had solidified her appreciation of the animal kingdom. She loved taking care of the dogs, cats, birds, and even reptiles. She would have liked to volunteer more often, but her parents didn't have time to drive her. Ian, her classmate who lived down the street, was the son of a veterinarian who volunteered at the shelter. They were able to give her a ride a few times.

Ian was one of the smallest boys in their class and it seemed like he tried to make up for it by being smarter than everyone else. He wore glasses and his clothes almost always looked new and unwrinkled. Even his handwriting was neat. He got all A's of course, and when kids weren't teasing him, they were trying to cheat off of his homework and test papers. When they were younger Ian was obnoxious, just like her little brothers. But Samantha and Ian had gotten to know each other last summer at the animal shelter, and now Samantha enjoyed talking to Ian.

Ever since she played with the dogs at the animal shelter, Samantha had been begging her parents to let her get a dog, but her mom said she was no longer accepting things that pooped or needed to be fed. Five kids was apparently her mom's limit.

Last summer Ian and Samantha sort of became friends, but once school started, she couldn't afford to be seen with him. He sat with a hodgepodge group of kids at lunch, and she sat with her boy-crazy friends. Ian didn't seem to be offended or sad when Samantha started cutting their conversations short. In fact, Ian always seemed pretty happy.

It was Samantha who kind of missed Ian. He always had some interesting factoid about animals to share or a cool story about how his dad the veterinarian had saved a real, live deer one time. It was way better than listening to Kayla fantasize about kissing her brother Jack with her new Petunia Pink lip gloss–*yuck!*

"The Native Americans were very protective of nature and took care to conserve it. Not like us today. There are 44 endangered species in Arizona alone. We have been poor stewards of the forests in northern Arizona and haven't done our part to respect nature," Mr. Turner lectured.

Ian blurted out, "Did you know there are only 45 Mexican gray wolves left in Arizona?"

Ian's knowledge of the animal kingdom seemed to be endless. He was very smart, and he confided in Samantha last summer that he was going to be a veterinarian just like his dad one day.

Mr. Turner replied, "No, I did not know that. Thank you for sharing that very sad fact Ian, but next time please raise your hand."

The teacher moved forward with the lecture and started discussing the Navajo war that lasted from 1846 to1863. Samantha did her best to pay attention but couldn't help noticing Bobby Lustin, the naughtiest kid in their class, put bright green gum under his desk. It looked like the glow-in-the-dark kind her little brothers liked. He glanced around to see if anyone saw his misdeed and made eye contact with Samantha. She quickly looked away and hoped he wouldn't cause any trouble for her.

The bell rang, signaling the end of social studies, and Samantha moved to health class. Ian walked with Samantha and yammered on about the Mexican gray wolf. It dawned on Samantha that she actually enjoyed listening to Ian. He was telling her about how he got to see a Mexican gray wolf that his dad saved last winter. The wolf was accidentally shot by a hunter, but the hunter did the right thing and brought the wounded wolf to Ian's dad. Ian's dad was able to save it, but it still had complications from the bullet wound. Instead of releasing it into the wild, the wildlife preservation professionals decided it should live in the local zoo. Samantha made a mental note to look for it during her next visit to the zoo.

As they walked into health class, Samantha veered away from Ian, as was her habit, and chose a seat in front of her pretty friends. They usually sat in the back of the classroom and tended to chit chat. Samantha actually liked to pay attention which is why she sat in front of them. She thought health was probably an important subject. After all, your health was something you'd have to live with for the rest of your life, right? Mr. Helm, the teacher, was droning on about the various fruits and vegetables that everyone should be eating for what seemed like an eternity. *Why do classes feel so much longer on Friday afternoons? Does time actually slow down?*

Mr. Helm paused and asked the class which important nutrient was found in bananas. Samantha's friends immediately filled the silenced pause with gossipy whispers.

I know this one. It's potassium. But then she second-guessed herself. *Or was potassium found in broccoli and magnesium found in bananas?* She was pretty sure that potassium went with bananas, but she wasn't willing to embarrass herself in front of the whole class just in case she got it wrong. Better to let someone else answer it.

Mr. Helm called on another boy that had his hand raised, and he said, "Magnesium."

"Nope," Mr. Helm said. "Magnesium is an important nutrient found in broccoli. Anyone else have a guess?"

Now Samantha was sure that potassium was the correct answer! She felt herself get warm with excitement… she was going to raise her hand… and then doubts crept in again. *What if you're wrong? What if people laugh at you? What would Ashley say about me answering questions in class? Would she, Kayla, and Emma call me a nerd?*

Mr. Helm paused for a moment and then sighed, "Potassium, potassium is found in bananas. And potassium is important for muscles just like magnesium."

Samantha had missed her chance, and she immediately regretted it. She should have raised her hand.

Before she got another chance to raise her hand, the bell rang. The weekend everyone had been impatiently waiting for was finally here. They shoved their books and school supplies into their backpacks and rushed to the door. Two days of freedom had officially started. Finally.

Samantha made her way outside and welcomed the fresh, almost-summer air. Every fiber of her being wanted to be out in the open. She looked at the bus, her usual transportation home, and her face scrunched up. It looked loud. There were kids throwing things and another younger boy sitting up front was wailing with his mouth open. Her two younger brothers, who were already on the bus, didn't seem to notice her.

Maybe it was something in the air. Maybe it was the thought of riding the noisy bus or going home to the chaos. Or maybe it was because she had nothing better to do with her Friday afternoon.

Whatever the reason, Samantha decided to walk home through the woods.

2

. . . .

Samantha had walked home from school a few times, but she had never hiked to her house through the woods. She was always too afraid. Sure, reading at her fort a few yards from her house was safe, but walking the entire two miles to her house seemed downright terrifying. Until today. Today was the day she would walk home through the woods for the first time.

Maybe Samantha was tired of being afraid. She was too afraid to raise her hand in social studies. She was too afraid to sit where she wanted at lunch. She was too afraid to wear the clothes she wanted, and was too afraid to walk through the woods. Well today, she was going to change one of those things.

Before she could chicken out and change her mind, Samantha walked fast to the edge of the forest. There was a small section of wood fence and a sign with a hiker on it designating the trailhead. She stopped and took a breath.

An energy was building up inside of Samantha that needed to get out. Her thoughts were racing, and she was feeling something. What? She didn't know. It was a combination of angst, impatience, anxiety, and some other stuff too.

She just needed to be somewhere peaceful right now and away from school, the noisy bus, and her always-chaotic home. As Samantha thought about her feelings, she realized she felt trapped. She always had to sit with Ashley, she had to wear certain clothes, she couldn't talk to Ian too much, and she couldn't look too smart or too dumb in class. The pressure was building up inside of her, and she wanted to run away from all of it. She needed to occupy her mind with new thoughts—a distraction. She'd rather be in the woods and free even though it was scary. It was better than feeling stuck like she had been all day.

A hike through the woods will be good for me. It'll be a new adventure, and I'll be able to do whatever I want. I can just be me for a while.

Samantha's house was on the other side of a large hill so all she had to do was hike up and down and make sure she headed west, well west by northwest. She had looked up the trail online many times and knew this was the path that would take her to her house. It was only two miles.

Samantha stepped into the woods with heightened senses. She tuned in to her surroundings and heard birds singing happily from branches up high. Looking ahead, the designated path was shaded by tall trees and hugged by thick bushes. Leaves were rustling in the wind, and up ahead a black crow cawed, probably about how lovely the woods were at this time of year. It hadn't snowed for a few months, and the days were getting longer. The spring air smelled like the promise of summer. School would be let out for summer break in a few short weeks.

She was in awe of the mysterious woods. On the weekends it was her refuge, and it was a comfort to her in times of stress. She constructed her reading fort to escape the craziness of her loud, large family, and she knew that part of the path—the short distance from her backyard to her fort—very well. She had walked it many times, even in the snow.

Samantha also respected the woods, sometimes out of fear. Even though the sun was shining brightly, the looming trees shaded all but a few piercing slivers of direct sunlight. The branches above and the bushes on each side were dense. While the path itself was clear of any dangers, Samantha wondered what could be hiding even a few feet off the path in the bushes. That was the main reason she had never walked the entire way from school to her house through the woods. She was scared.

Samantha's mother wasn't entirely against Samantha's affinity for the woods, but she wasn't entirely supportive either. As Samantha continued her journey along the forbidden path through the forest, her mother's words of warning popped into her head, "You just never know who could be lurking in there."

Last year a mysterious fire burned a part of the forest, and the fire department said an arsonist had started it. Since no one lived near that part of the woods, they suspected a homeless person was responsible but never caught the perpetrator.

Her heart beat faster, and she could feel her palms sweating. What would she do if a creepy person popped out from the thick underbrush? What if a fire started, and she couldn't outrun it? What if a snake slithered out from the bushes? She felt the fear rising up inside her, but she didn't want fear to ruin her Friday afternoon adventure. She was determined to stop being afraid of at least one thing in her life.

Besides, she didn't have another way to get home now. Walking through town would take forever, and the bus had surely left already. She didn't really have a choice—Samantha needed to get home. Her plan was to arrive home around the same time her brothers got home on the bus so that she wouldn't be late for dinner or get in trouble. In order to make that happen, she had to stick to the path and walk directly to her house. She tried to focus on her thoughts instead of her feelings, and she tried to stay rational.

I think I'd hear any weirdos before I saw them. And I'm pretty fast. I bet I could outrun most people. She decided to stay alert and listen for anyone rustling in the robust flora.

With new alertness and a determination to stay positive, Samantha walked resolutely through the woods. Her heartbeat returned to normal, and she found herself smiling at the pretty song of a bird up ahead.

This is what I needed—a beautiful walk through the woods where I can enjoy nature and clear my head. She reminded herself to enjoy her surroundings and to take it all in. She appreciated the many shades of green on the leggy evergreens, and the relaxing sounds of the various life forms that called the forest home. The trapped feeling, her stress, and the momentary fear were melting away.

Just as Samantha was assuring herself that a walk through the woods had been the right decision, she heard a louder-than-usual rustling in the bushes. Another concern of her mother's suddenly popped into her head. *What if I run into a bear?*

Samantha knew there were no bears in these parts of the woods, but she was prepared just in case she ever encountered a grizzly or black bear. Black bears were kind of like big dogs and talking in soothing tones while backing away slowly could protect you. Grizzly bears were different—and much more scary. The best thing to do if a grizzly bear showed up was to curl into a ball and look non-threatening. She had paid extra attention in Girl Scouts when they earned the Cadette Trailblazing badge as it seemed like information that was important to know.

A large, black raven flew out of a bush near where the rustling sound had originated. Samantha's shoulders relaxed again, and she picked up her walking pace to stay on schedule with her plan.

"I wish I had a dog," said Samantha out loud to no one in particular. A dog could hear and smell much better than she could. It would keep her safe. It would be like having her own bodyguard who was also a good friend. She could explore so many more places and have so much more fun if only her parents would let her get a dog.

After walking uphill for not quite a mile Samantha arrived at a fork in the path, and she wasn't sure which one to choose. The one to the left looked like it went southwest. She could see that the woods thinned and more sun reached the path. The one to the right looked like it went straight, due west as she had been traveling. It was also darker, had denser branches hanging over the path, and it sloped uphill. There was a large tree trunk blocking her way. It had moss on part of it, and she shivered to think what else might be growing or living in the fallen tree trunk.

Samantha stopped and considered her options. Heading due west over the tree trunk would be the quicker way to her house. She felt the fear creeping up to her throat. The left path looked so much lovelier. Maybe it would curve back around to the north eventually. *But do I have time to take that chance?* She wasn't sure, but the bus ride was probably about half way over for her brothers. She needed to hurry if she was going to make it home in time for her parents not to notice.

Samantha felt the doubts creep into her mind, just like they had in health class. *What if I choose the wrong way? What if I get lost? I'll end up getting home late, my parents will discover that I walked through the woods without asking, and I'll be grounded for life.*

She could hear them yelling at her already, "Samantha Grace! What were you thinking? You know the woods are dangerous! You could have been kidnapped by someone! Or eaten by a wild bear!"

In the end, her fear of her parents ended up winning over her fear of the gnarly, overgrown path. She knew she needed to move, and start walking uphill toward the fallen tree trunk.

She had made up her mind, but her feet still weren't moving in that direction. Apparently, the signals from her brain were having trouble making it all the way down to her feet.

Maybe the path to the right was only dark and scary looking for a little while, she thought. *And besides, I am being brave today. I am taking the first step toward being more adventurous. That's it. That's what the path to the right is—an adventure.* Maybe there was something spectacular at the top of the hill like an amazing view or something.

"It's an adventure," she said out loud to herself. And walked toward the darker, more mysterious, more interesting path to her right.

She managed to get over the trunk in her skirt without touching any nasty bugs and headed up the steep path. Despite the cool shade, Samantha was sweating after a few minutes of climbing. She wondered how far she'd gone. She guessed about ten minutes had passed since she'd been at the fork. The path had only gotten narrower, and the woods had only gotten denser. Her legs were covered in scratches from the imposing flora, and despite her best efforts to stay excited about her adventure, she was second-guessing her decision. She told herself to just keep moving. If she stopped, she knew her fear would get the best of her, and she'd probably turn around. She committed to walking for at least five more minutes. One foot in front of the other.

After a few more minutes of walking, Samantha saw light up ahead. It was as though the woods disappeared, and the sun was able to shine unencumbered to the forest floor. She quickened her pace and then stopped at the edge of a meadow.

The meadow was covered in wildflowers. It was beautiful. It was amazing. Samantha stopped, overwhelmed by the secret garden the woods had been hiding. Bees danced from petal to petal as the flowers swayed to the rhythm of the wind. On the far north side of the meadow, a young deer looked up at Samantha and froze. Samantha grinned, but didn't dare move any of her other muscles. She wanted to watch the deer as long as she could. After what seemed like a minute, the deer went back to eating grass, and Samantha slowly, noiselessly ventured into the sea of wildflowers.

The path through the meadow was still distinct—as though it had been walked over recently. She guessed that adult hikers must know about this place. Maybe there was a travel book called *Arizona's Best Kept Secrets* and this beautiful meadow was one of them.

Samantha couldn't believe how wonderful her adventure was turning out to be! A secret meadow, a deer; she was so proud to make it this far all by herself. Choosing the "scary" path and climbing over the tree trunk seemed like such minor inconveniences now. She was glad she'd made the decision to hike even though she was scared. Her mother had always told her, "Courage is just doing something even when you're afraid." Maybe her mother was right.

After the meadow, the path led Samantha back down the hill, and she easily made her way to the fort she built last summer. The three-sided fort was sturdy and made a good shelter on rainy days. It was her favorite spot for thinking and being alone.

The fort was only a quarter mile from her back door, and she jogged the rest of the way home, hoping that she'd arrive soon after her brothers. With any luck, no one would notice that she'd skipped the bus and walked through the forbidden woods without asking.

Instead of entering her house through the back door where her path ended, Samantha stayed hidden in the trees and walked past the neighbors' backyards. Then she headed east toward the opening of the cul-de-sac on Tolemac Way. It was where the woods met the sidewalk and the intersection was right by Ian's house. She would double-back by taking the sidewalk west to her house. This way she could enter through the front door as though she'd ridden the bus.

As Samantha exited the woods and entered civilization, she saw Ian swimming in his heated pool.

3

. . . .

Ian was an only child which meant his life had more amenities. He had his own room, the latest video games, and never had to wear hand-me-downs. He didn't have to wait until he was 16 to get his own cell phone either. His parents were often taking classes, working late, or on extended vacations which meant he was usually left unsupervised.

Ian noticed Samantha making her way to the sidewalk and shouted, "Hey, Samantha!"

He scrambled out of the pool and met her at the gate. He didn't let her in because the gate was secured by a lock, but they could talk easily enough through the bars.

"Were you hiking in the woods?" he asked incredulously. Ian was a few inches shorter than Samantha and had to tilt his head to look up at her.

She could tell by his tone of voice that he was concerned and also thought she was kind of cool for hiking through the woods. Ian was a cautious young man, just like Samantha, and wouldn't have ventured into the woods even if his parents didn't have rules forbidding it.

"Yeah, I hiked all the way from school."
Samantha said with a bright smile. Adrenaline from
finding the meadow was still pumping through her
veins. She realized immediately that blurting out her
secret to Ian was a mistake.

"But you can't tell anyone!" she said quickly,
hoping to undo her error.

If Ian told his parents and her parents somehow
found out, she wouldn't be able to visit the woods
anymore. *Ugh! Why did I just say that? I finally
worked up the courage to walk through the woods,
and now I may never get the chance to visit the
meadow or enjoy the peace and quiet again.*

"Why did you do that? Did you see any bears?
Mountain lions?" Ian asked.

Samantha laughed. "There are no bears near
this part of the woods. I didn't see any mountain
lion tracks either."

Samantha's face turned serious. "Ian, you can't
tell anyone, okay?"

Ian, still dripping water from the pool, gripped
two of the wrought iron bars and said in a serious
tone, "I promise I won't tell anyone. Who would I tell
anyway?"

Samantha breathed out a sigh of relief and
smiled, "Okay, thanks."

Ian said "Why did you do it though? Did you miss the bus or something?"

"No, I just didn't feel like riding the bus. And I don't know...I guess I was feeling adventurous today."

She paused and smiled. Ian smiled back at her.

"Well, I guess I better get home. I don't want my mom freaking out."

"Adios amigo," Ian called out as she walked away. She heard a holler and a splash as he cannon-balled into the pool.

Samantha walked down the sidewalk to her house with a smile on her face and then braced herself as she opened the front door. The house was loud, as always. Her two younger brothers were playing video games and squabbling in the den. Her mother was banging around in the kitchen, scrambling to get dinner on the table. She started yelling for someone to come set the table.

Samantha set down her backpack, walked to the kitchen, reached for seven plates, and started laying them out.

Will my mom notice that I didn't arrive with my brothers? Will she somehow notice that I'm sweaty and flushed from my hike? Samantha kept focused on her task and tried to keep her head down.

"Where have you been?" her mother asked.

"I walked home and then stopped to talk to Ian," Samantha said. It wasn't even a lie. She had in fact walked home and also stopped to talk to Ian. Her mother didn't respond and instead yelled for all of her siblings and her dad to come to the table. Samantha was relieved that her mom didn't scold her for walking home.

The rest of her family started making their way to the dining room.

Diana, Samantha's oldest sister and oldest sibling, was a sophomore in high school and was rarely without a boyfriend. She had already been taken to prom by one of the starters on the basketball team. Her outfits were always fashionable, her hair was always done, and she almost always got straight A's. She was as close to perfect as anyone could be.

Jack, the eighth-grade quarterback, was Samantha's oldest brother, but he was only one grade ahead of her. He was a student athlete, with an emphasis on the 'athlete' part.

Samantha's younger brothers, James and William, were in 5th grade and 3rd grade, respectively. They were mostly annoying and loud at this point in their short lives, although William, the youngest, could be a sweetheart sometimes.

Samantha's dad, Roger, appeared from the study. He had been in the army, but now he worked for the government and traveled sometimes. Samantha didn't exactly understand what he did, and it didn't matter. He was a great dad as far as Samantha was concerned.

Dinner was consumed in a loud and ferocious fashion. The younger brothers squabbled. Jack and Diana both vied for their parents attention by talking about all of the successes they had during the week. And Samantha barely noticed any of it. She was too busy reminiscing about her lovely afternoon in the woods.

After dinner Samantha silently slipped away from the busyness of clearing the table and disappeared to the room she shared with her older sister. She wanted to identify some of the flowers she'd seen in the meadow and wanted to find out the exact species of deer she had seen.

After a few minutes, Diana walked in and noticing the content on the computer screen said, "Are you going to spend your Friday night studying again?"

She said it with an air of disappointment and a touch of pity as though there was so much more to life than books and grades, and Samantha was missing out. Diana was convinced that boys, popularity, and looking good were the three ingredients to any female's happiness. And Diana just wanted Samantha to be happy. In her mind, Samantha must only be studying because she couldn't find something better to do on a Friday night. Diana did spend time studying to get her A's, but not on Friday nights. Friday nights were for socializing.

"I just had a few things to look up," said Samantha. "Hey, have you ever hiked in the woods behind our house?"

Diana was changing into a new shirt and then started gathering her purse and coat.

"Ugh, no!" said Diana emphatically. "It's dirty back there. And who knows what's hiding out there. Or worse *who* is hiding out there. Creepy!"

And with that Diana walked out to attend whatever very important social engagement was happening with her friends. Samantha sighed and turned to sift through the pretty photos on her computer.

Later on in the evening, Samantha's dad came in to check on her. He knocked first even though the door was open. Samantha turned and smiled, "Hey, Dad."

Her dad sat down on her bed and said, "Honey, are you doing okay? You seemed a little quiet at dinner. How was school today?"

"I'm good," said Samantha. "School was okay. I knew the answer to a question in class, but I didn't raise my hand again."

Her dad tilted his head. "Oh yeah?"

"It was in health class. The teacher asked what nutrient was found in bananas, and I knew it was potassium. But then I thought it might be magnesium so I didn't raise my hand."

Her dad smiled and patted her on the arm.

"Samantha, I know there is a brave, courageous young woman in there." He poked her arm and gave her a side hug.

"You just have to find her. Next time, I think you should raise your hand even if you're afraid. It's not a big deal if you say the wrong thing. And one brave decision can lead to another."

Samantha thought about her brave decision to walk home through the woods. Maybe that decision would lead to even more brave choices.

"Anyway, you'll get another chance to raise your hand. Life is full of second chances," her dad continued.

Roger paused and got a faraway look in his eye. Samantha guessed she was about to hear one of his old army stories. He often told rambling, vague stories about his time in the army. He never gave too many details, the stories were never gory, and Samantha never felt like she was getting the entire picture. The stories typically revolved around this lieutenant who had not only saved her dad's life, but also saved many men in their platoon. His nickname was Hairy Jerry because he had a reputation for getting his platoon out of hairy situations. He could also grow a beard in hours instead of days or at least that was how the legend was told.

Her dad's favorite army story was about Hairy Jerry and how he almost single-handedly thwarted an enemy attack. Roger's platoon was stationed on the front lines of a siege where the army had surrounded a fortified city. The citizens had not been able to import supplies for several weeks, and the army was expecting a surrender any day. The people in the city had stopped firing their weapons days ago so the army was safe and waited patiently for the siege to yield its desired outcome.

While the other American soldiers were relaxing, playing cards, and enjoying themselves, Hairy Jerry was suspicious about the city not surrendering. He couldn't sleep one night because it was bothering him so much. He suspected the enemy was receiving supplies somehow. In his estimation they should have surrendered days ago. Jerry knew supplies weren't being air dropped or transported through the city walls. And underground tunnels didn't seem likely since the army camp extended almost a mile from the wall on all sides. But on a hunch, Jerry walked out past the army camp and looked for holes or possible openings for underground tunnels. It was 03:00 hours and even the rowdiest soldiers were settled in for the night. The camp was silent as Jerry left to wander the empty fields surrounding the army camp.

A distant noise caught Jerry's attention and he went to investigate with his night vision goggles. He walked noiselessly through the sea of knee-high grass and soon saw human figures. He dropped to his belly and army crawled to get a closer look. He saw a man rise from the ground and then another. There were already half a dozen men standing nearby, and they appeared to be taking crates from the men who rose out of the ground. The crates were placed on a cart which was tied to a horse. *The city inhabitants were smuggling goods, but they were smuggling goods* out *of the city? What does the enemy have left to trade anyway?*

Jerry didn't know what to make of the scene. He watched until the cart and horse rolled away, and the men went back underground. He told his superior officer the next day, and a plan was put in place. That night after dark, all of the soldiers moved outside their camp, found the entrances to several underground tunnels, and waited. At 03:00 hours they were expecting the enemy to rise from their underground position. The plan was to arrest any men who exited the tunnels. Instead the army was surprised at what happened next.

The deserted army camp was suddenly lit up on all sides of the city. Several bombs and grenades went off at the same time, blowing up the empty tents, supplies, and vehicles. The soldiers were confused at first, but then realized the bombs and grenades were coming from a few dozen yards beyond them. The city inhabitants had been arming rebels of a neighboring city with weapons so the rebels could attack the camp and retake control of the fortified city. That is why the people had been smuggling supplies *out* of the city instead of receiving them—the crates were filled with weapons! Lucky for the soldiers, the rebels couldn't afford night vision equipment so they couldn't see the camp was deserted.

Because the platoon had moved to the outskirts of their camp that night, the rebels were within firing range. The soldiers quickly overtook the rebels, seized the weapons, and stopped the attack on the empty camp. Once the residents realized the rebel attack was thwarted by Jerry's curiosity, they surrendered the city. Because of Jerry, the army didn't lose a single soldier during the rebel assault, and he was hailed a hero. Her dad clearly admired him and had fond memories of Hairy Jerry.

Instead of telling his favorite story, tonight Roger started reminiscing about a second chance he had received in the army.

"Once when I was in the army, I had to make a split-second decision like that. I was in an intel meeting, and I had some information that wasn't confirmed. I was very junior at the time and didn't want to waste anyone's time with misinformation so I kept my mouth shut. But then I couldn't sleep that night so I told my platoon leader the very next morning. We ended up investigating the intel and sure enough it was good intel."

"See? There's always a second chance."

He kissed her on the top of her head and left.

Samantha wasn't exactly clear on the details of her dad's story, but she was sure he meant well. She not only loved her dad, she liked him too. He was a great listener, and he usually knew what to say to make her feel better. Even though his story didn't entirely make sense, she understood his meaning.

There really will be a next time. And gosh darn it if she wasn't going to raise her hand next time!

4

Saturday morning was the time Samantha's family set aside for chores, and the entire house needed to be cleaned with everyone's help. Samantha's assigned chore was cleaning the bathrooms. Usually Samantha would lay in bed as long as she could, linger at breakfast, and then procrastinate. Scrubbing the bathrooms in Samantha's house was not for the faint of heart. If there was a contest for ickiness, she was certain her three brothers would win first place.

On this Saturday Samantha woke up early, ate breakfast, and scrubbed the bathrooms in record time. Today she cleaned with the energy of a girl on a mission. There was no time to stop and reflect on the filthy bathrooms–she was going on a hike.

She finished with everything before Diana woke up and had to quietly choose her outfit for today's adventure. *No skirts!* She put together a hiking outfit made of boots, cargo shorts, and a t-shirt. She decided to fill her backpack with a peanut butter sandwich, apple, nuts, and water so that she could spend all day in the woods.

Her mom entered the kitchen and Samantha had to explain why she was packing a lunch on a Saturday.

"I'm going to spend all day at my fort," she said.

"Are the bathrooms cleaned?" her mother asked skeptically.

"Spic and span," replied Samantha cheerily.

"Okay, well, be careful. Don't stray too far. You never know what wild animals could be out there," her mother warned. "And make sure you're back before dark."

Samantha escaped to the backyard through the sliding glass door. She breathed in the fresh morning air, and it smelled like freedom. She reveled in it. Samantha felt like a new person, like she had conquered something by walking through the woods. And then she realized she had conquered something—her fear of the woods!

What other fears could she conquer? Unfortunately, Samantha's list of fears was long. She was afraid to answer questions in class, she was afraid of getting into a confrontation with Ashley, she was afraid of not having any friends, she was afraid of spiders and bees, and she was afraid of heights too.

A few years ago, she wanted to jump off the high dive board at her swimming lessons. She was standing on the high dive trying to work up the courage to jump when a naughty kid climbed the stairs after her and jumped on the board while she was on it. The board wobbled, she lost her balance, and fell the entire way to the water. She could still remember the panic in her throat and how it seemed like she was falling for a long time. Raw fear stifled her screams. The only thing she heard on the way down was laughter, the laughter of Bobby Lustin who had wobbled the board. Even now she could hear his laugh clearly—it was so imprinted in her brain. She hit the water sideways with her right thigh hitting the water first, and her ribs following shortly thereafter. The wind was knocked out of her. As she sank to the bottom of the deep end, she couldn't breathe and somehow even more panic filled her body.

As she'd struggled to swim up toward the light, toward the air, she was certain she was going to die in that pool, but the lifeguard jumped in to save her. Other than a deep purple bruise on her right thigh, no permanent damage was done... physically. She had never gotten over her fear of heights and even now thinking about it made her hands shake. She rarely thought about this unpleasant event, but when she did, it made her feel scared and thankful to be alive. Today she felt a new feeling when she ran the memory reel in her head—she felt anger. She was angry at Bobby Lustin for causing her to fall. He was banned from swimming lessons that summer, but never apologized or showed any remorse. At school, Samantha went out of her way to avoid him. He, however, seemed to have forgotten about her and hadn't done anything mean to her since then.

A raven cawed overhead and broke Samatha's reverie.

Why am I thinking about that terrible day? I should be excited about today! I get to go exploring through the woods. She brought her thoughts back to the present and took a good look at her beautiful surroundings.

She felt older and more mature as she walked. And she was filled with anticipation. What new adventure would be waiting for her today? Maybe she could make friends with the raven. She knew that ravens could learn to recognize human faces and would sometimes even bring shiny objects to humans as gifts. *That would be so cool!* Maybe she would see the deer again. Or maybe she'd be able to get close enough to feed it her apple. Her happy thoughts carried her quickly along the path.

As Samantha approached the final stretch to the meadow, she heard a high-pitched noise and immediately stopped. Her mother's warnings flashed in her brain, "Those woods are filled with all sorts of dangers."

The sound couldn't have been made by a man so it couldn't be a weirdo. She wasn't sure what bears sounded like, but it sounded too small to be a bear. Snakes didn't make noise. As her brain searched for other terrifying things that make noise, she heard it again. It was almost like a whimper. It sounded like a dog.

Samantha knew about the dangers of wild dogs. When she volunteered at the animal shelter she had seen all of the worms, fleas, and other diseases wild dogs and cats could have. She proceeded cautiously with heightened senses and heard it again.

It definitely sounded like a dog. And it sounded like it was coming from a large tree up ahead. She stood still and focused on her curiosity until it grew bigger than her fear.

She walked slowly and cautiously off the path toward the sound. She climbed over a bush, around a tree, and saw it.

Laying on the ground was a puppy like creature with a bloody leg. It was crying and didn't seem able to move.

Samantha's first impulse was to rush to the animal and look at its leg. She felt instant sympathy and compassion for it. But she knew better than to make sudden movements around new animals, especially wounded ones.

Samantha froze.

And then she whispered, "it's okay" in a sweet, gentle tone, and slowly lowered herself to her knees all the while cooing at the injured pup.

Samantha wasn't quite sure what breed of dog it was. Maybe it wasn't a dog, maybe it was a coyote. Coyotes were common around here, and she had never seen a coyote pup so she wasn't sure.

The animal, whatever it was, started scooting away from Samantha and crying louder. It was almost howling now, and Samantha started to get nervous.

What if its mom comes back and it really is a coyote? Samantha would definitely be in trouble then. How could she get it to stop crying? Food. Animals always appreciated food.

Samantha took the peanut butter sandwich from her backpack, broke off a piece, and placed it in front of the pup. She scooted back to let the animal know she wasn't a threat. It started sniffing the air and then inched toward the white bread sandwich. The puppy ate it quickly, and had to work to get the peanut butter off the roof of its mouth.

It was so cute and innocent. *Ugh, why won't my parents let me have a dog?*

When the puppy had cleaned out its mouth, it looked at Samantha.

"Do you want more?" Samantha asked in a gentle tone. She broke up the rest of her sandwich and fed it to the animal in pieces. It ate the whole sandwich and then looked up at Samantha again.

Samantha only had an apple and nuts left in her lunch. She didn't think that dog like creatures ate either of those so she fashioned a water bowl out of the plastic bag and brought it close to the creature's nose. It sniffed her hand suspiciously, sniffed the water, and then it drank.

Samantha felt a small wave of relief wash over her. It was learning to trust her, and maybe she could actually help. After it drank, the pup rested its head in exhaustion. Samantha didn't know what to do, so she sat down next to it and stroked its head until it fell asleep. After it was breathing deeply and steadily, Samantha quietly adjusted herself so she could take a closer look at its leg.

She cautiously leaned toward the wound and saw a deep gash running the length of the leg. It was dirty and leaves were stuck in the dried blood. She wondered if the leg was broken too. It wasn't pointing in the wrong direction and there were no obvious bones sticking out, but a fracture would be hard to see. The wound needed to be cleaned and bandaged. She didn't know if she would be able to sneak into her own house and confiscate the necessary supplies without someone noticing.

Samantha decided she had to try and help the wounded animal. It wasn't really a choice. The animal could either die or Samantha could try to save it. As she walked back to her house, she started making a list in her head. *I'll need hydrogen peroxide, bandages, more food, a water bowl, tweezers to get the leaves out... what else, what else?* She hadn't done this before; she wasn't sure what she was forgetting.

After Samantha made it through the rear sliding glass door, she walked immediately to her room with her backpack. If she could take the items she needed and bring them one-by-one to her room, maybe she could smuggle out the supplies without anyone noticing.

The first task of her mission was to get into the bathroom. The downstairs bathroom was occupied by Jack. When she knocked on the door and asked how long he was going to be, he just yelled, "Leave me alone!"

Samantha headed to the upstairs bathroom. Her sister was in it, and was apparently giving herself an extreme makeover. There were cotton balls, nail polish, curlers, irons, and makeup covering every inch of the counter. When her sister saw Samantha walking toward the bathroom, Diana shut the door in her face.

Great! Now, what am I going to do? She went back to her room to gather herself and come up with a new plan. She had some money saved; maybe she could get to a drugstore. But how would she get there?

Then she thought about the poor helpless creature. She couldn't let it die a horrible death of gangrene or whatever other infection it might catch outside in the dirt. She thought about the wounded animals that Ian's dad had treated at the animal shelter last year. She couldn't remember all of the steps he'd taken to treat open wounds.

Of course! Ian will be able to help with the puppy! He'll know what to do!

Samantha grabbed her backpack and headed down the street to Ian's house. She wasn't sure what excuse she was going to use when Ian's parents answered the door. She'd have to think of something quick. Maybe she could tell them that she needed help with homework.

She took a breath and rang the doorbell. After a beat, the door opened. It was Ian.

Samantha blew out a sigh of relief, "I'm so glad it was you that answered the door."

Ian smiled. "What's up?"

"I need your help. Are your parents home?"

"No, my mom plays tennis and my dad plays golf on Saturdays. They won't be home until late."

Samantha strode into the house, "Good! We are going to need bandages, hydrogen peroxide, tweezers, and meat, and I'm not sure what else."

She headed for the bathroom and Ian followed closely behind, "For what? What's going on?"

"I found a hurt puppy in the woods." She couldn't hide the concern in her voice.

"Whose puppy? How did it get hurt?"

"It's not anyone's puppy. It's a wild dog. Well, I'm not even sure if it's a dog," Samantha said. "It might be a coyote. And it has a hurt leg. It's all bloody and has a big gash. I have no idea what happened to it. But I think its mother might have abandoned it. It was crying and crying for who knows how long."

Tears welled up at the thought, and she had to stop talking. She turned away to hide her watery eyes and started opening cabinets and drawers to pull out what she needed.

"Can we take these?" she asked, holding up some gauze bandages.

Ian stared at her with a furrowed brow, a symptom of the debate taking place in his head. He wanted to help, but the woods were forbidden. And neither he, nor Samantha was qualified to take care of a wounded animal. But his parents weren't home, and they weren't old enough to drive the animal to a vet. So what choice did they really have? After a pause, he said, "Yeah, if it's an open wound, we really have to clean it out. The peroxide should do the trick."

Samantha grabbed the gauze, tape, hydrogen peroxide, scissors, and tweezers from the bathroom and then headed downstairs.

Ian had gathered a paper dressing gown from his dad's black bag. Samantha also noticed an open backpack and a plastic sandwich bag of mystery meat sitting next to Ian. He was putting on some shoes.

Samantha felt some of the tension in her shoulders release. She had help and felt very lucky to have Ian on her side. With Ian, his dad's supplies, and some luck, maybe they could nurse the helpless creature back to health.

"Thanks for helping me," she said with sincere gratitude. Ian smiled back at her and nodded.

"It'll be an adventure," he said. Silence filled the air for just a moment until Samantha remembered one more thing.

"Oh, we need a water bowl too," she said. They grabbed a few water bottles and a shallow plastic bowl and hurried off through the woods.

5

Samantha and Ian both stopped when they reached the tree. Samantha held her breath and walked slowly around one side. The crunching leaves under her feet had never been so loud. And her heart felt like it could beat right out of her chest. She peered around the trunk and saw a leg.

The puppy is still here! But then she realized the leg wasn't moving. And she couldn't hear any whining. What if she had taken too long getting the supplies? What if the puppy hadn't made it?

She sucked in a breath and took a step so she was standing in front of the tree. The pup wasn't moving. She leaned down as a sob rose up in her throat. *Please don't be dead. Please don't be dead.*

As she knelt she saw the pup's chest rise up and down just a little. And then she noticed its leg twitch. It was still alive! It was just sleeping.

Samantha looked up at Ian with relief and whispered, "It's still alive." And beckoned for him to come see it.

The animal woke up at the sound of Samantha's voice and whimpered happily. Samantha pet its head, and the pup licked her hand with mild enthusiasm. It remembered her!

Ian walked to the back of the tree and froze. He was just staring at the wounded animal and not moving. Samantha looked back at him as she mouthed, "What?"

"That's a Mexican gray wolf!" Ian said a little too loudly. The pup got scared and tried to retreat without much success. The pace of its breathing increased and became ragged.

Samantha put her finger to her lips and gave Ian a harsh look. Ian's shocked expression turned meek as he mouthed, "Sorry."

Samantha slowly turned to the supposed wolf and murmured at it. She looked at the animal more closely. It did have larger than normal ears and it was gray. Maybe Ian was right. She couldn't worry about that now. Whatever type of animal it was, they needed to get the wound cleaned and bandaged.

Samantha gestured for Ian to hand her his backpack. First, they needed to get the animal off the dirt. She pulled out the paper dressing gown and laid it down right next to the wolf.

She was talking to the pup while she did this hoping to keep it calm. The creature was too sick and tired to move very much anyway. "Ian, help me lift it onto the paper."

Ian still hadn't found his voice, but dutifully went to the wolf's backside and helped Samantha lift it onto the paper. The pup yelped, but only wiggled a little. The poor thing was not doing well.

Ian and Samantha both saw the dark purple puddle of blood where the pup had been laying. It was a miracle the pup was still alive. They looked at each other and Ian said, "I'm not sure if hydrogen peroxide and bandages are going to be enough."

He looked older and more mature when he said it. Ian saw the harsh reality wash over Samantha and he immediately felt sad that he delivered the bad news so soon. But he also didn't want Samantha to get too attached. He had seen animals at his dad's office lose less blood and still pass away.

Samantha wasn't sure what to do next. Should they try to feed it? Or should they start with the bandages? She took out the meat and tried to get the pup to eat. It was already asleep again though. *That can't be good.*

"I guess we should do the bandages first," Samantha said in the most matter-of-fact tone she could manage.

They used one of the water bottles to rinse the injured leg. Washing away the dried blood opened the wound, and it started bleeding again. The wolf woke up but barely protested. Samantha shoved the water bowl near its face, and it drank a little. Ian was working on the leg, picking out the bigger leaves and pine needles with his fingers. "I don't think its leg is broken," Ian said.

"Are you sure?"

"No, we would need an X-ray to be sure, but I don't see any compound fractures. The bones aren't sticking out or anything like that. I guess we'll find out when… or if it starts walking again," Ian said.

"Maybe we should call my dad," he continued. He started reaching for his cell phone.

"No!" said Samantha in a harsh whisper. "Then my parents will know that I broke the rules, and I'll be grounded forever. And what will they do with the wolf pup? What if I never get to see it again?" Tears were welling up in her eyes.

"I guess there isn't much more my dad could do anyway," conceded Ian. "Well, besides the X-ray. But if it does live, we'll know pretty quickly if the leg is broken or not." He sighed.

"How about this? If it lives, but it can't put weight on the leg, then we call my dad," Ian suggested. "If it's not walking a little bit by Tuesday then we'll tell my dad."

Samantha agreed. It was a good deal, and probably the best one she was going to get. "You won't tell anyone until Tuesday?"

Ian nodded solemnly. "If it even makes it to Tuesday."

Samantha looked at him with sadness in her eyes. She didn't want to think about that outcome. *Stay focused on the task at hand* she told herself.

Ian moved aside. Samantha pulled out the tweezers and carefully removed all of the little pieces of debris. *This is kind of like the game Operation.* Samantha was so focused on her goal she wasn't grossed out or anything. All she could think about was saving the baby wolf.

Ian turned on the flashlight in his cell phone and shined it on the pup's leg to help Samantha be as thorough as possible. They both knew leaving dirt in the wound would lead to infection and any infection could be a death sentence.

Once Samantha finished her task with the tweezers, she looked at Ian for his approval. He grabbed the hydrogen peroxide and offered it to her with raised eyebrows. Did she want to pour the pain-inducing, but necessary liquid? Samantha grabbed the hydrogen peroxide with her left hand and placed her right hand on the pup's side. Ian moved to the wolf's head and gently placed his hands on the small animal too.

Samantha took a deep breath and poured almost half of the bottle onto the bloody leg. The pup yelped and writhed in pain. It even tried to bite Ian with its baby teeth. Ian and Samantha both stayed steady and held it in place. The wound was oozing with white bubbles, a sign the solution was working.

Samantha splashed one last bit of peroxide on the wound, and they both waited for the animal to calm down. It didn't take long. The poor thing was so weak.

Next they needed to wrap the leg in bandages to keep it clean. Ian cut the gauze pieces and handed Samantha the tape while she carefully wrapped the leg. It wasn't a skillfully wrapped bandage, but it would definitely keep the dirt out. The wolf was asleep or passed out again and didn't complain as they carefully moved its leg into a resting position.

Samantha knew the animal needed to eat and she tried her best to wake it up. It ate one bite of the meat. *Better than nothing, I guess.* Ian refilled the water bowl and left it for the wolf. Samantha was going to leave the meat too but Ian thought other animals would smell it.

Samantha sat down next to the pup and petted its head. "I'm going to have to think of a name," said Samantha as she stroked its head.

Ian stood up, looked at Samantha, and paused.

"What?" asked Samantha.

With sympathy and concern in his eyes, Ian said, "Maybe you should wait a few days before you start thinking of names."

Samantha looked at the innocent creature and cried. She didn't even know why she cared so much about this little wolf she had only met this morning, but she did. She didn't want it to die. Seeing it laying there, looking so small, she knew Ian was right. The young wolf might not survive the weekend.

Ian sat down next to Samantha and waited quietly. She managed to pull herself together, wiped her eyes, and looked at Ian.

"When do your parents get back?" she asked.

Ian's parents were going to be home any minute, and Samantha would have to leave for dinner soon too. Ian headed off first while Samantha stayed another hour to say goodbye. It was just an animal. This is the circle of life. Death was natural. At the animal shelter, she knew some animals had to be put down. It was just the way things had to be. But not this animal. This animal was hers now. This wolf needed to live.

She stroked its head and coaxed the wolf into eating one more bite of the meat before she reluctantly tore herself away and ran home. Tears streamed down her face as she ran. She wiped her wet cheeks, and took a deep breath to compose herself before she walked through the rear sliding glass door.

6

Thankfully dinner was late at Samantha's house that night and no one noticed her off-schedule arrival. Samantha's thoughts were a million miles away until her dad mentioned that there was going to be a hard freeze tonight.

"Imagine that! Having to cover the garden in late April?" he said.

Samantha realized the wolf didn't stand a chance of making it through the night unless she did something.

She went through the motions of the evening without enthusiasm and her perceptive dad noticed. "What are you thinking about Samantha?" her dad asked.

"I was just thinking about my day in the forest," Samantha said. "Do you think it'd be okay if I walked home through the woods after school?"

"Well, I don't see why not," her dad said. "It's only a few miles, and you're old enough to handle that. It would be good exercise for you."

His response made Samantha very happy. She was glad her dad trusted her so much. She went to bed on time but lay awake with her thoughts solely focused on the wolf.

Diana's bedtime was 9:00 pm, a full hour later than Samantha's. Diana slept with her earbuds in, and Samantha could hear her breathing heavily by 9:30. Tonight, Samantha wasn't even interested in sleeping. She just wanted to get a warm blanket to the wolf before…before anything bad happened. After lying in bed for what seemed like an eternity, she was finally confident that her parents were asleep too.

Samantha's feet touched the ground without a sound, and she managed to grab her winter coat and shoes without disturbing Diana. She went to the fridge, took whatever was left of the meat, and pulled an old blanket from the basket next to the couch. She figured no one would miss it since it was all ratty and torn anyway, but it was fleece. The fleece would keep the wolf nice and warm. She silently opened the rear sliding glass door and deftly walked through her backyard to the woods.

Once she reached the denser part of the woods, Samantha realized she forgot a flashlight. Luckily, it was a full moon tonight, and moonlight traveled from the cloudless sky to her path unencumbered.

As she arrived at the tree, she strained around the trunk to see the pup. The outline of a large lump came into focus. It was much bigger than the pup. She held her breath and listened. *What could it be? Could the mother have come back? Was it another animal?*

Samantha froze until her curiosity grew stronger than her fear. She moved closer.

It was a blanket.

Had Ian come back with the blanket? Is that something a friend would do? Lend a helping hand when it was needed? Samantha knelt down and cooed at the wolf. Its breathing was steady and gentle. That had to be a good sign, right? Samantha spoke softly, "Hey there, sweetie. I brought you some meatloaf."

The wolf raised its head and looked at Samantha. *Another good sign.* Samantha put the meatloaf near its mouth, and it ate hungrily. Then Samantha stayed with the small animal, stroking its head until it fell asleep.

She quietly got up, walked back to her house, and shoved the fleece blanket into the bottom of the blanket pile. She took off her coat and shoes, and managed to get back to bed without anyone noticing. She lay awake staring at the ceiling.

It's still alive. It might actually survive the night. What am I going to name it? And then she remembered Ian's words of warning.

Maybe on Monday, she'd think about names. Right now, she needed to get to sleep so that she could wake up early. She turned on her side and fell into a fitful sleep.

On Sunday morning, Samantha quickly changed into hiking clothes and ran to the large tree. Ian was there already. "How's it doing?" she asked.

Ian looked at Samantha with a serious face. Samantha felt a wave of worry hit her stomach.

"I can't tell," said Ian. "I guess it looks better. It was trying to stand a while ago. But it's just weak."

"Have you been feeding it?" asked Samantha.

"Yeah, it finished the steak I brought today, and the milk too," said Ian. "And then it went to sleep."

"Milk? Good idea!" said Samantha. "I didn't even think of that." She sat down next to the animal and stroked its head.

"Well, that's good, right? If it's eating then that means it's getting better, right?"

"Probably." said Ian. "The good news is that I saw it put some weight on the wounded leg. I can't be sure, but it didn't look broken."

Ian stood and brushed the dead leaves from his shorts.

"I have to get back home," said Ian. "If my parents ask, I was at your house this morning, okay?"

"Yeah, okay." Samantha said distractedly. She looked up at Ian who was now standing, "I'll see you tomorrow."

Ian turned and walked off toward his house.

Samantha realized she had forgotten to thank him for bringing the blanket last night. In the light of day, she could see it was a drab gray blanket. It looked coarse and old and reminded her of a blanket she had seen in one of her dad's army photos.

Samantha made a mental note to thank Ian tomorrow. She sat there with the wolf most of the day while it slept and only woke to eat occasionally.

7

....

Samantha's parents told her she was allowed to hike back and forth to school as long as she walked her brothers to the bus stop first. "Family comes first," said her mom. "And you're responsible for making sure your brothers get to the bus stop safely."

On Monday morning, Samantha was anxious to leave the house, and tried to hurry her little brothers. Excitement welled up in her and she even allowed herself to hope a little. Today was the day she would get to name her wolf...maybe.

She put some extra meatloaf in her lunch and practically shoved her brothers out the front door. She walked them down Tolemac Way to the bus stop. It was right in front of Ian's house even though Ian didn't take the bus. When the yellow bus arrived, she said goodbye to her brothers. James was too busy climbing the bus steps to acknowledge her but William gave her a happy wave and a cheery goodbye.

On the bus, she could see Bobby and his older brother teasing one of the older kids in the back. Thankfully, her little brothers were too young to draw the Lustin boys' attention. Bobby was the youngest of the Lustin boys and once he graduated, the middle school would finally be free of the dreaded Lustin gene pool.

Samantha shook her head and felt bad for the kid being teased, but as the bus pulled away her attention shifted to this morning's mission. She took off at a trot. The walk to the pup seemed long this morning, and soon her trot turned into a jog.

As she approached the tree, she saw the blanket in a heap. She pulled the blanket back to uncover the wolf, but it wasn't there. It was gone.

"Oh no," she said out loud and sat down on the hard ground. She ran through all of the possibilities in her head.

Maybe a bigger animal had come and eaten her wolf. Maybe the mom had come back and taken it away. Maybe it had dragged itself off and died somewhere nearby. She had heard that dogs like to be alone when they know they're going to die. But maybe, just maybe it had survived the night and was off exploring.

That was the best option, Samantha decided. *I'll hope for that.* She got up, looked around, and started walking around the tree trunk in progressively larger circles. And then she whistled. Softly at first and then louder. If the injured animal had somehow gotten up and moved away, she wanted to make sure it heard her.

I wish they would have taught us tracking skills in Girl Scouts. She looked for baby paw prints on the ground, but the forest floor was mostly covered in pine needles and leaves. There weren't any blood trails or any other kind of trail for her to follow.

Samantha whistled for what seemed like forever but was probably only minutes. The birds sang back to her, but her young wolf didn't appear. She didn't know what to do. Should she leave the meatloaf even though it might attract another animal? Should she give up? Should she come to grips with the fact that the pup was gone for good?

She sat down and sighed. And felt the tears rising again. Her chest tightened and she stifled a sob. *What am I going to do now?*

Then she heard a rustling in the leaves. She looked back up the hill, past the tree where the blanket was still laying and saw the wolf hobbling slowly toward her. The bad leg was still wrapped in the excessive bandage, and the young creature seemed to be managing with it. Despite its haggard appearance, the wolf seemed to be in good spirits and increased its pace when it saw Samantha.

Samantha stood up and covered the distance between them. She picked up the gray wolf, and it licked her face. Samantha laughed and was overcome with relief to see her wolf had survived another night. She didn't want to put it down, but it was wiggling, and she didn't want to exacerbate its injury. She gently put it down on the forest floor and sat down. The wolf sniffed her backpack and Samantha laughed as she fed it the leftover meatloaf.

The wolf ate all of it. Samantha refilled its water bowl and then had to leave for school.

"I'll be back before you know it," she told the animal. "I am going to spend all day thinking up the perfect name for you, and when I come back this afternoon, we'll see if you like it."

It was difficult for Samantha to leave her new friend, but she had to go.

As she traveled the rest of the way to school, she thought of different names. Should she choose a person's name like Lucy or Tracy or should she go with a dog name like Spot or Buster? Ian would help her, hopefully.

She was late to homeroom, but Ian had saved her a seat. He was literally sitting on the edge of his seat and had an anxious expression on his face. She smiled at him and mouthed, "It's fine." He grinned at her and relaxed back into his seat.

After homeroom on their way to social studies, Samantha gave an update on the wolf's health. Ian asked if the bandage was soaked through with blood or not. Samantha couldn't remember if it was white or red, but didn't remember seeing red or feeling anything wet when she picked it up. Ian said that they should change the bandage after school tonight anyway.

Samantha remembered to thank Ian for bringing the blanket out to the fort on Saturday night, and Ian looked at her nonplussed, "I didn't bring that blanket."

He said, "I thought you did."

Samantha said, "I didn't do it. Who else could know? Did you tell anyone?"

"No, of course I didn't tell anyone," said Ian defensively.

"Weird. I wonder where it came from. It kind of reminds me of a blanket in one of my dad's old army photos," Samantha said. "Who could have brought it out there?"

Samantha wondered if her dad had followed her out to the forest. But that wasn't possible. He had worked on Saturday and Sunday mornings. And Samantha couldn't picture her mom going out into the woods. Her mom was like Diana and had a very strong aversion to dirt.

Ian shrugged. He hadn't told anyone and didn't know anyone with an old army blanket.

"Well, I guess I should just be happy that the wolf is okay," said Samantha. "What should I name it? Will you help me come up with a name?"

"How about Rambo?" said Ian.

"Eww, no," Samantha laughed. "Besides, what if it's a girl?"

"Oh right," said Ian. "We forgot to check over the weekend. We should check after school."

"How can we check when it's still so young?" asked Samantha. She knew from working at the animal shelter that most mammals had to be at least two months old before you could tell. She suspected the wolf was six weeks old at most based on its size. But of course she wasn't an expert. And neither was Ian. They were just figuring out things as they went.

"My dad showed me," said Ian. "Girls have two holes in the back and boys only have one."

Samantha stifled the urge to giggle and just smiled instead. Ian was very serious, but it felt weird to be talking about animal holes.

"Okay, well what if she is a girl? What should I name her?"

"I don't know," said Ian. "All I know is that if it's a boy you should definitely name it Rambo or the Terminator."

Samantha gave out a "hmph" and rolled her eyes. *I guess I'll have to come up with the name myself.*

When lunch rolled around, Samantha grabbed her lunch and then looked at her usual table where Ashley and her friends sat. Ashley returned her gaze and smiled like a lion about to feast on its prey. Ashely was, no doubt, mulling over Samantha's promise to revisit the idea of a sleepover. Samantha's gaze moved to the other side of the cafeteria where Ian sat with his friends. The hodgepodge group was chatting lively and appeared to be having a good time. One of the math club members, Jenny, caught her eye and waved for Samantha to come sit with them. As Samantha walked toward the group, she recognized another boy from band and another girl from her science class. She didn't know their names, but with the wave from Jenny and her adventure with Ian this weekend, Samantha felt sure she'd be welcome.

Samantha headed toward Ian's group and sat down next to Jenny. After a quick and friendly "hi" pointed in Samantha's direction, Jenny's attention returned to Ian and Jeremy's lively discussion about a rare breed of ants. Jeremy, also a math club member, was talking about his uncle who shipped rare ants to certain Asian countries for $400 a box. The ants were only found in southern states in the US and apparently were needed for some sort of scientific experiments in Asia. *Fascinating! What else do these people know?*

"How do they keep the ants alive?" asked Samantha without thinking. She was new to the group and probably should have waited and watched to figure out the social rules of this group before she spoke up. *Who was the prettiest? Who was the leader? Who did she need to pretend to be to fit in?* But it was too late. The words had just slipped out—her curiosity had once again resulted in impulsiveness. She felt her face flush as she waited in fear to be judged, talked over, or ignored.

Jeremy turned and looked at her, "I actually don't know. They probably FedEx them overnight in special containers or something." The conversation turned to a trending YouTube video that everyone in the entire world, except Samantha, had apparently watched last night.

Samantha reflected on her impulsive question. This group oddly didn't seem to care that Samantha was new to the group, or that she was wearing a long skirt instead of a short one. She didn't feel judged, and she didn't feel pressure to become someone she wasn't. Samantha took a breath and relaxed. Being popular all of a sudden seemed like a lot of work. Maybe she was better off with Ian's group of friends.

As lunch progressed, Samantha found herself enjoying the time and not wishing for the bell like she usually did. She didn't get her typical anxious stomach ache either.

The bell rang and Samantha was bummed. She wanted to keep talking and hanging out with Ian's friends. She got up reluctantly and started walking to social studies with Ian and Jeremy. Jenny was in the GATE program so she went to a different classroom after lunch.

In the hallway, Ashley, Kayla, and Emma started walking right behind Samantha whispering and giggling. When Samantha turned to see what was going on, they immediately stopped and just looked at her. Ashley's eyebrows raised as if to say, "Wouldn't you like to know what we were talking about?" And then she smirked.

Samantha felt her heart beat faster and her palms started to sweat. She was afraid. She was afraid that Ashley would yell at her or be mean to her or do something awful. She felt like she should apologize for offending Ashley. Maybe an apology would protect her from Ashley's wrath.

"Sorry I didn't sit with you at lunch," said Samantha. "I just had to talk to Ian about some stuff. Is it still okay if I sit with you guys during social studies?"

Ashley brushed past Samantha and gave her a dirty look. Kayla tried to copy Ashley's facial expression, but didn't look nearly as mean. She stalked after Ashley. Emma's eyes got big and an apologetic look washed over her face as she mouthed, "sorry" to Samantha. She sheepishly followed Kayla and Ashley into social studies.

Samantha sat next to Ian and Jeremy in social studies. She felt bad, like she had done something wrong. Choosing Ian over Ashley had clearly offended Ashley and complicated things. Were Ashley, Kayla, and Emma still her friends? Or had her deepest fears just come true? Was she now all alone in middle school? How long would Ashley punish her? Samantha started thinking up ways she could make it up to Ashley. And then she started thinking about whether or not she really wanted to be Ashley's friend anymore. Was being alone all that bad?

Bobby made a noise that pulled Samantha from her reverie. He came from a long line of troublemakers and dutifully upheld the tradition his two older brothers had started. The Lustin boys were well known for being tardy, disrespectful of other people's property, and just downright mean. And the older they got, the worse they behaved. The oldest Lustin, who was in Diana's grade, had gotten in trouble for doing donuts on the football field with his Camaro and messing up the expensive turf. Jimmy, the Lustin brother in eighth grade, had been caught spray-painting 'SCHOOL SUCKS' on the back of the school. It was like they were all competing to come up with the dumbest way to get in trouble. Bobby's clothes were tattered, his hair was greasy, and he had written all over his shoes and arms with ink pens. Samantha was scared of Bobby and avoided all the Lustin boys as much as she could.

Today, Bobby was clearly amused with himself for something. His gaze was focused on a beetle that he no doubt had placed in Elizabeth's open backpack right on top of her social studies book. Samantha was about to say "watch out," but Elizabeth had already reached down to grab the book. As her hand touched the beetle, she screamed, jumped out of her seat and danced around beside her desk. Her red, curly hair was bouncing everywhere as she jumped about. The room fell silent except for Elizabeth's "eews" and "grosses." And then Bobby started chuckling. Causing trouble seemed to be the only thing that brought the Lustins any true joy.

Elizabeth stopped her frenzied bouncing long enough to point and yell, "He put a beetle on my book!"

The rest of the class started looking on the ground for the beetle. Many of the girls squealed in second-hand horror and lifted their feet off the floor just in case.

Mr. Turner was watching the show with a dispassionate expression on his face. He sighed, looked at Bobby over the bridge of his glasses, and handed Bobby the red card for detention. Bobby took it and then walked out of class whistling, like he was glad he'd gotten in trouble.

Ian managed to chase down the beetle and captured it with a paper cup and piece of paper. Mr. Turner suggested that Ian toss the beetle out of the window, and that's what he did. Soon social studies was back to normal and Mr. Turner resumed teaching them about Native American life.

Samantha's thoughts drifted back to lunch. *Did I do something wrong?* She thought about Bobby's bug stunt. Bobby had clearly done something wrong. His intent was malicious, and he behaved disrespectfully. *Is sitting with another group of people at lunch malicious? Is it disrespectful to Ashley?*

Maybe Ashley was the one behaving immaturely in this situation. The more she thought about it, she realized she hadn't done anything wrong. Samantha should be allowed to sit with whomever she wanted at lunch. And if Ashley couldn't handle that and needed to be mean to Samantha because of it, that was her choice. But Samantha didn't think she needed to apologize for sitting with a different group of people at lunch. She had a lot of feelings to sort out, but didn't want to think about it right now. She decided to focus on the teacher and learn even more interesting facts about the Navajo people.

Mr. Turner paused during class to collect his thoughts on something, and Samantha could hear her potentially former friends using the pause to giggle and whisper. She was almost certain she heard her name mentioned in the mischievous gossip. She redoubled her efforts to concentrate on social studies and noticed that Ian and Jeremy were taking notes just like she was.

After social studies, she walked with Ian, Jeremy, and their friends to the next class, and then she sat with them. And that's how the afternoon went. She wasn't alone, and she wasn't part of Ashley's clique anymore either.

It was like Samantha had just decided to take a new path through middle school. It was scary. Ashley might be mean to her, but right now, it felt like a weight was lifted from Samantha's shoulders. She felt a little more free and maybe even walked a little taller.

Ian, Jeremy, and their other friends were all accepting of Samantha. They included her in conversations and were genuinely nice. *I should have done this sooner!*

8

As soon as the final bell rang Samantha and Ian scurried into the woods. The same woods that filled Samantha with terror just three days earlier now seemed benign and friendly. As they reached the fallen tree trunk, Samantha showed Ian how to maneuver over it. And when the meadow appeared in front of them, Ian stopped and just said, "Whoa!" The deer wasn't there today, and there wasn't any time to stop. Samantha dragged Ian through the flower field, and they finally made it to the tree trunk where the blanket was still laying.

Samantha tried whistling but she was breathless from running. Ian caught his breath first and let out a whistle. They heard distant rustling, and then the pup appeared. It was still hobbling, but looked happy.

Samantha rushed to it, and they happily greeted each other as though they were lifelong friends reuniting after years of separation. The pup licked and whined and Samantha laughed as she pet it.

"Wow! It looks great!" said Ian. "We should take care of that bandage though." It was spotted with red where the blood had soaked through.

"Can we check to see if it's a boy or a girl first?" Samantha asked. She was anxious to name it.

"Sure," Ian said.

Samantha pointed to the ground and said, "Lie down." But the pup didn't understand. Ian walked over and started rubbing its belly even though it was standing. The pup understood and immediately lay down, eager for its first belly rub.

Samantha took over the belly rubbing duties while Ian inspected the back end. He moved the tail out of the way and examined the animal with the seriousness of a skilled and seasoned vet. Ian looked up at Samantha with the best poker face he could manage.

"It's a girl?" Samantha asked through her laughter. "A boy? What is it? Tell me, Ian!"

Ian sighed. "It's a girl," he said, feigning disappointment as his head dropped in defeat.

"Woo hoo!" said Samantha.

She took the pup's head in her hands and said, "I am going to name you Sasha. What do you think of that?"

Sasha licked her nose. Samantha laughed.

"I think she likes it," said Ian.

They played with Sasha for a little bit and tried to teach her to sit and lie down. Then they worked on replacing the bandage around her leg.

Samantha lifted up the gray blanket to look for the paper dressing gown they used yesterday, but it was gone.

"Sasha, what did you do with the dressing gown?" Samantha asked. That was weird. First the blanket appeared out of nowhere and now the dressing gown had disappeared.

"We don't need it," said Ian. "We can just put her on the blanket instead. It doesn't look like the wound is bleeding much anyway."

Sasha wiggled and yelped when they poured the hydrogen peroxide on her leg this time. She was much stronger today. In fact she almost escaped their grasp, but Ian managed to hang on tight.

"Hey, girl," said Samantha. "It's okay. We have to do this to keep the infection out. It'll only sting for a minute." And Samantha pet her until Sasha calmed down.

Once Samantha finished wrapping the bandage, it was time for both of the middle schoolers to head home. Samantha exited the woods and entered through the rear sliding glass door now that she didn't have to keep her afternoon hikes a secret.

9

. . . .

Sasha healed as the weeks passed. Samantha and Ian made it a habit to walk to and from school whenever possible to play with Sasha and check in on her. Ian's parents had agreed to let him hike in the woods as long as he stayed with Samantha and had his cell phone.

Soon the school year was getting ready to end and Samantha couldn't believe how much her world had changed. Samantha now sat with Ian's group of friends regularly at lunch. She wore shorts and t-shirts to school, and she raised her hand in class all the time. Her grades had always been good, but now teachers knew her name and even called on her sometimes when there was a tough question no one else could answer.

Ashley responded to Samantha's disloyalty with classic mean girl tactics. Ashley gossiped about Samantha, spreading rumors about how Samantha was a "nerd-lover" and telling everyone she had a crush on Ian. Kayla and Emma dutifully followed her lead giggling and whispering about Samantha on the walks to class and even during class.

Samantha responded to their immaturity by ignoring them as her mother always suggested. "Just ignore them. They'll get bored and go away."

But after a few weeks of ignoring them, they were still coming up with derogatory things to say about her clothes and about Ian. Samantha was sick of it. Being "friends" with those girls and making peace was no longer an option, and she was fed up with their antics. One day after lunch, as they were walking to class, Samantha heard them whispering and giggling about her. She was pretty sure she heard them say something about how Ian's brain must have been God's way of apologizing for making him so small. And that was the final straw.

Samantha stopped in the hallway and turned to face Ashley and her goons. A few of the other kids, including Ian, lingered to watch the confrontation. Samantha summoned her courage, took a deep breath, and turned to face her former lunch crew.

When she had their full attention, Samantha started out softly, "Ashley, I think my decision to sit with a different group of people at lunch hurt your feelings. Is that right?"

Ashley made an indignant sound, but didn't say anything. Samantha continued, "I'm sorry if I hurt your feelings. I didn't mean to hurt you, but I think I have the right to sit with whomever I want at lunch. Don't you think so?"

Ashley stared at Samantha with round, blue eyes, and then she gulped.

"Could you please stop spreading rumors about me? If you have a problem with me, just tell me to my face, okay?"

Ashley started turning red and then she gulped again. Kayla and Emma were clearly uncomfortable.

One of the kids who had lingered yelled, "Oh man!" But the climactic confrontation was less dramatic than expected. They all turned and walked to health class. Ashley was unusually quiet during class that day, and Samantha didn't hear any more gossiping from Ashley for the rest of the school year.

Samantha's life outside of school was transformed as well. Samantha used to spend her evenings and weekends cooped up in her room trying to ignore Diana's many phone conversations. Now Samantha spent all her free time in the forest. She was living two lives, one at home and one in the woods.

Sasha's leg was mostly healed and she could run easily. The young wolf was strong and growing quickly. Even when Samantha ran as fast as she could, the wolf always ran faster. They would race up and down hills where the trail was smooth.

They frequently ended up at the meadow where Sasha would try to play with the deer. She was still too small to be considered a threatening predator, so the graceful deer would sniff her and then nonchalantly amble away no matter how energetically Sasha entreated it to play.

Samantha spent time with Sasha after school almost every day. Ian came when he was able, but being an only child, he didn't have as much freedom as Samantha did. His parents tended to care when he was gone, except when they were on vacation or pursuing their many hobbies.

Sasha was smart and quickly learned when Samantha was due in the woods each afternoon. Sasha would track her scent and meet Samantha early on the path. Instead of sticking to the clearly marked path through the woods, Samantha started exploring the woods with Sasha.

With Sasha by her side, Samantha felt like the entire forest was her playground. Sasha was smart enough to sense danger and her heightened senses allowed her to smell and hear any danger before Samantha could.

One day while they were racing up a hill, Sasha came to a dead halt and growled at a bush off to the side. When Samantha came over to inspect the apparent danger, she saw a snake coiled up in the bush. Sasha became her protector. And Samantha wasn't lonely when she was with Sasha. Sasha became her friend too.

When Ian hiked with Samantha and Sasha they became braver still. They explored almost every inch of the forest going east and west over the hill.

On the weekends, their hikes stretched further north into the woods, into unknown territory they had yet to explore. One Saturday afternoon they walked quite a long way to the north and stumbled across a blackberry bush planted next to a babbling brook. The berries were still green as summer was just starting, and the water was basically melted snow.

Her mother's warnings still lingered in the back of Samantha's mind, but they seemed dim and mostly irrelevant with Sasha nearby. When she was with her friends, Samantha was quite sure that weirdos, hunters, bears, fire, and any other potential peril in the woods weren't a danger to her.

Sasha began hunting her own food—rabbits, squirrels, birds, and other small animals. And since they had found the creek near the blackberry bush, Samantha stopped filling the water bowl. It had mysteriously disappeared anyway. Samantha wondered if Sasha was in the habit of digging holes and burying things. She knew dogs did that, but did wolves?

On the Saturday before the last week of school, Samantha and Ian roamed the woods with Sasha. They headed further northwest than they had before. Sasha had grown a lot and was able to cover longer distances now. They followed the creek and walked along its winding curves.

Samantha heard a low murmur in the distance, and they headed toward it. As they got nearer, Ian became convinced it was the sound of rushing water. They climbed over a summit, and then they saw it—a giant waterfall with a pool of crystal-clear water at the bottom. The waterfall was on the north side of the pool, and it was big. Samantha guessed it was as tall as a two-story building. Vines hung down from the cliff and framed the cascading water.

The south end of the waterfall was the exit point for the pool—this was the start of the stream they were following. The head of the stream had giant, flat rocks on either side which looked perfect for sitting or sunbathing.

It looked incredibly inviting on that warm summer day. Ian and Samantha decided to jump into the cold water at the same time. Despite their lips turning blue and the incessant shivering, they were both laughing and splashing.

Sasha wanted to join the fun, but was incredibly nervous and kept pacing along the water's edge, whining. Samantha laughed, "Who's the chicken now? Come on Sasha! Come here girl."

Finally, Sasha made her move and half jumped, half slipped into the refreshingly cold water. They played in the water for what seemed like minutes, but must have been hours.

Ian got out and climbed partway up the big black rock that made up the west wall of the pool. He was poised to jump. It looked too high to Samantha.

"Ian, don't do it," said Samantha. "What if the water isn't deep enough?"

"It is. I already checked," said Ian. "Plus, from up here I can see how the colors change. The deeper water is darker. It's totally safe. Watch me!"

He got a running start and jumped! He grabbed his legs in the classic cannonball position and hit the water with force.

There was a big splash and Samantha let out a scream. When Ian didn't surface right away, she took in a deep breath. She wasn't going to panic yet, but she started counting. By the time she counted to three Ian resurfaced. He was elated and laughing.

"That was awesome! You have to try it, Samantha. It is so cool. You just have to make sure your butt hits the water first."

"Hah! I don't think so," said Samantha. She told Ian the abbreviated version of her high dive experience and about her fear of heights.

"Okay, I get it," said Ian as he floated on his back and made the occasional lazy backstroke. "I would be scared too."

Samantha stiffened at the word *scared*. She didn't like being described with that word. She wasn't scared anymore. She had decided to make new friends, walk through the woods, and for heaven's sake, she was friends with a wolf! She wasn't scared.

And yet, as she thought about climbing up and jumping off the black rock, scared was exactly what she felt. But could she do it? Maybe. Would she land sideways again and hurt herself? Maybe.

Samantha decided that today she wasn't ready to jump off the same high rock, but maybe she could try a smaller jump first. Maybe she could work her way up to it. She was sure they'd be back at this pool again, so she'd have some time to start practicing. She started surveying the rocks around the pool trying to find a shorter one for her first jump.

"What time do you think it is?" asked Samantha.

"Huh, well where's the sun?" said Ian. He shaded his eyes and looked toward the west, where he had just jumped off the giant black rock. It was shiny and slippery from water splashing on it.

"Hey, do you see that?" Ian asked.

"See what?" Samantha asked.

"I think it's a person." Ian pointed to the very top of the western cliff. The man was backlit by the afternoon sun so they could only see an outline of his shape. He was tall and broad-shouldered. His beard was full and his hair was long. The outline of his clothes revealed their tattered edges. He was close enough to hear Ian but didn't seem concerned. In fact, he seemed unusually calm. He slowly turned and walked out of their view.

"We'd better go," said Samantha trying to keep the panic out of her voice. Her mother was right. There were weirdos in the woods! Goodness knows how long he had been standing there. And what else had her mother been right about? Were there hunters too?

They scurried out of the water and put their shoes on. Sasha was peacefully drying on a rock in the sun and rose to follow them as they quickly headed southeast back to safety, away from where the man had been standing. Sasha didn't seem overly concerned with the situation—she hadn't snarled at the man or barked.

"Some guard dog you are," muttered Ian under his breath.

Samantha heard him and didn't necessarily disagree with his snide remark. She had been trusting Sasha to keep them safe. Maybe Samantha shouldn't assume Sasha would be the bodyguard she'd expected.

As they scurried out of the area surrounding the watering hole, Sasha stopped and started sniffing the ground.

This is no time to linger. But then Samantha saw the bright green thing on the ground. It looked very out of place in the woods where all of the colors were muted shades of brown and green. Samantha stopped and bent down to look at Sasha's discovery. It was a piece of gum—bright green gum, just like the glow-in-the-dark gum Bobby had put under his desk.

Was Bobby Lustin hiking through the woods? He didn't seem like the nature-loving type so what could he be doing out here? There weren't any girls to tease and no walls to graffiti, although he did manage to litter. What typical behavior from a Lustin. They didn't respect anything.

"Bobby Lustin chews that kind of gum," said Samantha. She looked at Ian with wide eyes.

"Well that couldn't have been Bobby at the watering hole. That was a grown man, not a kid," Ian reasoned aloud.

Samantha suddenly didn't have a good feeling about being this far out in the woods anymore, and she hurried to catch up with Ian.

They hiked for a minute or two and then Sasha started sniffing the air. The smell had her full attention as she stopped in her tracks. And then without warning, Sasha took off at a full sprint. Ian was so dumbstruck he just turned to look at Samantha, but Samantha was already sprinting after Sasha.

Samantha ran as fast as she could and wasn't even thinking about spraining her ankle or worried about how she was going to get over the tree trunk that was up ahead. For some reason the smell of a campfire popped into her mind. She pushed the thought away. There was only one thing to focus on right now. *Run faster*. She caught glimpses of Sasha and knew she was still heading in the right direction. Suddenly she saw Sasha take a defensive stance. *Was Sasha growling?*

Samantha had never seen Sasha display such aggressive behavior before. Maybe there was a guard dog in Sasha after all. Samantha slowed down and approached the scene hesitantly. Samantha was suddenly very aware that Sasha was a wild animal capable of wild animal behavior. She got to the clearing and saw what Sasha was growling at.

It was Bobby.

10

Bobby Lustin was standing frozen beside a small fire he hadn't meant to start. He wanted to explain it was an accident, but the words wouldn't come out. Not that Samantha would believe him anyway. He thought back on the events that led him to this uncomfortable and dangerous position.

Bobby's morning started like usual. He was awakened prematurely by the amplified sounds coming from his brother's guitar. His mom, who worked two jobs, was gone and his dad didn't seem to be home either. His three older brothers had eaten the last of the cereal. He managed to find a granola bar in the back of a cupboard, but was still hungry after he ate it. Jared, his oldest brother started yelling at him to clean the kitchen, and then Jimmy started punching his arm for no reason. Hungry, tired, and fed up with his brothers, Bobby decided to get out of the house. He wandered into the forest with his slingshot, a magnifying glass, and his favorite treat—a fresh pack of glow-in-the-dark gum. He could buy it at the mini-mart by their house for less than a dollar, and it helped quell his hunger.

He walked for hours, practiced shooting at targets with his slingshot, and eventually stumbled on an ant hill. He knew a magnifying glass could focus sunlight into an intense ray that could burn the ants, but he'd never tried it. It took a minute or two to tilt the glass at just the right angle, and then the ants started withering, smoking, and dying. He meticulously worked his way around the hill, trying to kill every ant. He was so focused on his ant eradication, he didn't notice the dry leaves next to the ant hill starting to smoke. By the time he realized his careless mistake, a wolf appeared a few feet away from him and started growling. He was too scared to move, and the fire was left to grow.

A few seconds later, Samantha arrived panting and out of breath.

Why didn't it look like a campfire? she thought. Samantha realized the fire wasn't surrounded by rocks to keep the fire contained. And it was growing taller, consuming the leaves under a small bush where it had started. The bush stood alone, but sparks were flying off of it, and Samantha instinctively knew they were all in a very dangerous situation.

Samantha immediately pulled off her backpack, took out her water bottle, and poured it on the base of the fire just as she had been taught. It helped. In fact, most of the flames were gone now. But the fire wasn't entirely out. And even if there weren't flames, Samantha knew that hot smoldering leaves or wood could restart the flames quickly.

Bobby started stuttering what sounded like excuses. Lame excuses, Samantha was sure. But Samantha just yelled over him, "Ian!!! Ian!!!"

She needed more water. She'd have to go get more water from the watering hole. It was the closest source since there weren't any hoses or faucets in the middle of the woods. She yelled at Sasha and Bobby to stay and took off for the watering hole.

"Ian! FIRE!" she screamed. She was almost hoarse now from the smoke and from the yelling. She passed Ian as she sprinted to the watering hole. Ian was bewildered, but Samantha managed to yell, "Fire!" and pointed toward Sasha.

Ian had a bigger water bottle than Samantha, but she wasn't sure it would put out all the new flames that had probably rekindled. She had to get more water, fast. She needed a plan. What was she going to carry the water in when she got to the watering hole? She had her water bottle but nothing else. And then she remembered a scene from a movie where she saw the actors beat down a fire with a wet blanket. But she didn't have a blanket. *Why didn't I think to grab Ian's shirt?*

As Samantha approached the watering hole, what she saw once again jolted her to a halt. The trim, broad-shouldered man was kneeling by the watering hole holding a gray blanket under the water. He raised his head and with a deathly expression on his face said, "Did you yell fire?"

Now wasn't the time to be scared of the strange man. There was no time for feelings. The fire was probably spreading.

"Yes!" Samantha managed to choke out a response. She watched him pull the saturated blanket from the water and heave it over his shoulder. It was clearly heavy, but he moved with ease and in fluid motions. He was lean, but unusually strong.

"Show me," he said as he started jogging toward her.

And without a second thought, Samantha took off sprinting again. Even though the man was older, older than her dad, he was right behind her. He kept up with her the entire way to the fire. They smelled the dark gray smoke before they saw it. Just as Samantha feared, the flames had spread to the next bush and were quickly growing.

Sasha stood guard by Ian who turned to look at Samantha with wild eyes. Bobby was standing next to Ian, and the moment he saw the man with the blanket enter the clearing, fear took over his face.

The mysterious man spent no time getting to work. He threw the blanket on the ground and stifled the entire fire in moments. Then he lifted the blanket, flipped it, and threw it on the charred ground.

They all gaped at the man's strength and grace. He moved quickly and precisely until the last of the embers were drenched.

With the fire gone, Samantha tried to take a deep breath, but ended up coughing on smoke. She knew the threat of resilient flames still lingered in the ashes.

Ian and Samantha turned toward a commotion in the forest—someone was running. They realized Bobby was gone. The old man shook his head in disgust. "This is the second time I've had to chase that kid out of the forest after he started a fire."

Samantha realized that Bobby must have been the arsonist who started the forest fire last year.

The old man turned to face them and said, "Start throwing dirt onto the charred ground." He didn't say it with anger. He didn't say it with frustration. He said it with authority.

Samantha and Ian both hopped into action and immediately started shoveling dirt onto the charred ground with their hands.

"I'm going to get another blanket and some more water, the man said. Samantha thought she heard him mutter "it's going to be a long night" as he took off at a quick jog.

After the old man was out of ear shot, Ian asked, "Was that the man from the watering hole?"

"Yeah, I guess he heard me yell *fire*. He was already at the watering hole dunking that blanket in the water. Did you notice the blanket?"

Ian tilted his head as if that would help him remember. He shook his head.

"It's the same kind of blanket we found on Sasha the night it froze," said Samantha.

Maybe the strange man wasn't so strange after all.

They continued to throw dirt on the ground and even had to stomp out small flames occasionally. The old man arrived with a large jug of water and the blanket he had drenched for a second time. He laid the soaked blanket on the hottest ground and then stood and looked at the seventh graders.

"What's your name?" He looked at Ian first and then Samantha.

"I'm Ian."

"I'm Samantha."

She paused and then followed up, "What's your name?"

He looked at her and smiled. He didn't show teeth; he didn't break into a full grin. It was just a slight uplift of both cheeks and some extra wrinkling around his eyes. Eyes that were full of kindness and something else, maybe sadness. "Gerard."

Sasha headed to Gerard and greeted him. Gerard knelt down and rubbed Sasha's head. They clearly knew each other.

"It was you," said Samantha. "You gave Sasha the army blanket."

11

. . . .

After a long pause, Gerard finally nodded and said, "That's right. You are the ones who saved her life though. She would have died long before night time if you hadn't stopped the bleeding and cleaned her wound."

Samantha had so many questions. Where did this man come from? Why did he have an army blanket like her dad's? And why was today the first time they were seeing him? They had been roaming the woods with Sasha for months now! Surely they would have seen this man.

"Do you live close by?" asked Samantha instead.

"I do. I've lived in these woods for the last few decades; I live in an abandoned mission just up the hill," Gerard replied. "I've been keeping an eye on you three to make sure you didn't wander too far or get yourselves into trouble. I guess I should have been keeping my eyes peeled for that Bobby kid instead."

"You live in the woods? Why?" Ian asked with innocent curiosity.

Samantha thought she saw Gerard's expression turn sad, but then he gathered himself. "Well, it all started when I got out of the army. I was pretty restless after I was discharged so I decided to go on a bit of an adventure. I knew about a gold treasure that some settlers supposedly buried in these hills. The story had always fascinated me so I decided to go on a treasure hunt."

"Did you find it?" Samantha and Ian asked in unison. It was just like Mr. Turner's stories! Maybe there really was gold buried in these hills.

He chuckled at their enthusiasm. "No, not yet. But I haven't given up entirely. I'm just taking a break and enjoying myself for a while."

They were quiet for a beat, and then Ian said what Samantha was thinking "Well… we are studying some stories about lost gold in school. We might be able to help if you want."

Gerard grinned at them. He wasn't in the habit of accepting help from children, but their naïve hope reminded him of a simpler time in his life. A time when chasing down a hidden treasure seemed possible. He remembered what it was like to believe in a future full of potential and possibility. There had been a time when he was ready to take on the world and willing to see the best in it.

The real reason Gerard moved to the woods all those years ago was because the people he loved had been taken away from him. On one terrible night his whole world was shattered, and he felt he couldn't handle life anymore. After losing everything, he started to view the world around him through a new lens. He became extremely disappointed with society—the politics, news, media, stock market and everything else. It was all too much for him to handle along with his broken heart. He couldn't stand to be a complicit participant anymore. He couldn't handle the stress. And he deliberately chose to leave it all behind.

Living in the woods and living off the land was simultaneously his silent rejection of society and a tribute to the Native Americans who came before him. His lifestyle mirrored theirs in many ways, except he lived in an abandoned mission instead of a cliff dwelling. But he lived off the bounty of the land by harvesting deer and small animals for food and making sundries out of the carcasses. He kept a small garden and his clothes were either very old and tattered or made from animal hides. His water source was the waterfall which he boiled before drinking, although it was so clean and his body was so used to the water, he probably didn't need to anymore.

Gerard's simple life more or less consisted of the same routine until Sasha—and subsequently Samantha and Ian—had stumbled into the woods a few months ago. His afternoons and weekends were now spent watching over them from a distance.

"Well that sounds like a great idea," Gerard said. "I can use all of the help I can get. Would you like to hear the story of how I learned about the gold in the first place?"

Samantha and Ian both found a comfortable place to sit and glued their attention to Gerard. Slowly, he started the story he knew by heart. He was enjoying himself, and it was a pleasure to finally share the story with people.

"When I first moved to the woods to begin my treasure hunt, I knew about two settlers from Spain who struck it rich when they hit a deep gold vein. The settlers were two brothers, Alfonso and Fernando Saez. They heard about an Apache tribe that was coming to attack them and take their gold so they split up. Alfonso, the older brother, went out to meet the Apache. He took the guns and dynamite and laid out booby traps for the Apache. Fernando went to hide the gold, and then he joined Alfonso in the fight. Both of the brothers died in the attack, and the Native Americans never found the gold. I was told that this story took place in the 1860's, but I couldn't be sure."

Samantha and Ian both started asking questions at the same time. But Gerard held up a hand. "It's getting late, and you've both had a lot of excitement today. I think it's time for you to head home. Besides I need to dunk this blanket again and keep an eye out for smoldering embers."

Gerard knew the dry leaves were a hazard that would need to be watched for many more hours. "Why don't we meet at the watering hole tomorrow, and I'll show you the journal I found about the treasure?"

Samantha and Ian both wanted to protest, but could see by the position of the sun that dinner time was approaching. They both agreed to meet him in the morning and headed home.

The next morning, both seventh graders and Sasha were at the watering hole early. Gerard was already there and appeared to be munching on some sort of meat that was dried into jerky.

Gerard sensed Ian and Samantha's excitement and after saying hi, he dove right in to the rest of his story.

"I didn't have much to go on. There was a poem published in the newspaper that was reported to be from one of Fernando's journals. The poem is supposed to be directions to the buried treasure. This is what was published in the newspaper about 30 years ago."

Gerard handed over a worn-out piece of newspaper. The paper was thicker than a modern newspaper, but the text was very faint. They could barely make out the passage:

To my brother Alfonso, the end is near
*   I feel heavy and sad, full of fear*
If by some chance you do survive
*   Go find the gold and live your life*
Walk on water, climb the wall
*   Trust the creepers, you will not fall*
Look for Saez, the treasure's within
*   Dig brother dig, let your new life begin*

"That was it. No one knew how to decipher the poem to get a location," Gerard said with a bit of sadness in his voice.

"What does he mean '*walk on water*'?" asked Samantha.

Ian shrugged, and Gerard said, "I don't know."

Gerard continued, "It wasn't until a year later that I found the next clue. When I first moved to the woods, I spent most of my time much further north of here, but a few years ago, I was wandering south and stumbled across the mission. I started reading the books in the library to pass the time. And one day I came across a journal from Fernando Saez. It was too much of a coincidence to not be the same Fernando Saez. Little by little I combed through all of the journals in the library looking for clues or a record of the hidden treasure, and one day I found this."

He handed a worn, leather book to Ian and Samantha peered over his shoulder to read it with him. They saw the poem. It was the same poem, but it had more lines! The sloppy writing was big and had likely been written in a hurry.

To my brother Alfonso, The end is near
I feel heavy and sad, full of fear
If by some chance you do survive
Go find the gold and live your life
Pass our friend who hibernates
Be quiet and sly, don't tempt the fates
Follow the path to the well
Where we listen for the bell
Renew your strength with running water
Pass the home of swimming otter
Walk on water, climb the wall
Trust the creepers, you will not fall
Look for Saez, the treasure's within
Dig brother dig, let your new life begin

Above the poem was a paragraph, also in Fernando's handwriting. The ink was faint, and the cursive was intricate and neat. Samantha read the paragraph out loud, slowly.

"My dear brother Alfonso, I fear you may be dead at the hands of the Apache already, and I might never see you again. If you do survive the attack, and I am not here, these clues will lead you to our treasure. You know the path well. You know the place."

Samantha looked up at Ian and Gerard with wide eyes. *What did it all mean?* It was like an inside joke between two brothers, a shared language only they could understand. How were Ian, Gerard, and Samantha going to figure it out?

"Hmm… ," said Ian thoughtfully. "Maybe we should take each verse by itself and try to unravel the clues one by one."

"*'The friend who hibernates'* might be a bear," said Samantha. "Gerard, do you know of any bear dens?"

"I haven't been able to find even one of the locations Fernando writes about," said Gerard. "I haven't come across any bear dens, wells, otters, or places to walk on water. I know these woods like the back of my hand, and I just don't know what Fernando is talking about. It's like all of the locations have disappeared with time."

"That makes sense," said Ian. "Whatever bell they were talking about probably doesn't work anymore. If there was a bear den back in 1860, then it's probably not a bear den anymore. And I know for a fact that otters no longer live in Arizona. Maybe the well is filled in by now, and maybe the creepers, whatever those are, are gone. All of the clues are going to be different now." He heaved a defeated sigh.

"But some things in the woods would still be the same," said Samantha. "I mean certain rocks and trees are more than 150 years old, right? And just because a bear doesn't actually live in the den anymore, maybe something like a cave still exists." She didn't want to give up the treasure hunt before they even started. They had the whole summer ahead of them. Surely they could make progress and figure out some of the clues at least.

Then Samantha had an idea. She paused. "Gerard, have you read through the rest of the journals to try to find geographic clues? You know, like landmarks?"

Gerard's eyes went wide. "No, I haven't. That's a great idea! We should look for references to rocks, trees, and geographic anomalies that could help us find the locations."

They both got up and looked at Gerard expectantly. "Well, follow me, I guess," said Gerard. Gerard had never had company at the mission before, but sharing his beloved journals with these two hopeful, energetic youths seemed like the next obvious step in his revived treasure hunt. He hadn't had this much fun in years.

Gerard was happy Ian and Samantha had found him, but the hope and happiness he was feeling inevitably reminded him of his happy past life before it shattered on that one fateful evening. He pushed the memories into the back of his mind and tried to stay focused on the present.

The front of the old mission had stood the test of time. It was still white, the wood doors were still in place, and the obligatory bell still hung in an arch above the doorway. It was weathered and parts of the side walls had crumbled, but it was very much a solid-looking structure. Although the area around the mission had been cleared of flora and fauna at one point in time, the last century and a half allowed nature to reclaim the land surrounding the mission and even parts of the building too. Vines crawled up the walls of the mission, and overgrowth hid all the pathways leading to and from the mission. The mission was barely visible from even 20 yards away because the trees and bushes were so thick.

Gerard opened the unlocked front door and Sasha followed him with obvious familiarity into the mission. They ambled into what looked like an old library. Dusty books covered the walls from floor to ceiling, and a wooden desk that looked too heavy to move took up a large portion of the small room. Ian and Samantha were anxious to get started on the research.

Ian found the section of the library where the matching brown leather journals were all shelved together. He grabbed one and gave it to Samantha, "Here you go!"

Ian grabbed a book for himself. They sat down and quietly, carefully started reading every line of each journal.

"They say something here about a tree," said Samantha. "But I don't think it can help us. It just says that the tree is big and beautiful."

They sat enraptured in their journals, each deciphering Fernando's 150-year old cursive as best they could. Occasionally they would comment to one another about a bush, a rock, a hill, but none of the scenery descriptions they found seemed to be distinct or helpful. They stayed until the long shadows were too large to ignore any longer.

"We need to get home," said Ian.

Samantha looked at him and nodded. And then she looked at Gerard and stuck out her lower lip to make a sad, pouty face at him. It reminded him of a little girl about Samantha's age he used to know a long time ago. He chuckled even as his heart clenched at the memory.

"I'm going to keep reading," said Gerard. His homemade candles sat in old clay candle holders around the library.

"And we'll come back tomorrow," said Samantha. It was summer after all, and they were free to hike in the woods every day now.

"Would you be so kind as to escort us home, Sasha?" asked Samantha while stroking the wolf's head. Sasha leaned into Samantha's hand. The three of them headed south through the woods. They stopped at the patch of burnt ground where they had fought the fire yesterday just to make sure it was still safe. The charred ground looked free from embers, although Samantha did notice a fresh new piece of bright green gum littering the ground. Apparently, Samantha and Ian were not the only ones who were curious about yesterday's crime scene. They kicked some extra dirt on the black ground just to be safe. Samantha dutifully picked up the green chewing gum, and wrapped it in the bag that had carried her lunch. Bobby Lustin was gross, and his discarded chewing gum was even grosser, but she couldn't let the littered gum sit there.

When they reached the tree line behind Samantha's backyard, she petted Sasha and said goodnight to both of them. Sasha and Ian continued on to Ian's house.

Before Samantha took the final steps toward her back door, she looked back carefully at the woods. She felt like someone or something was watching her and took a minute to listen for the crunching of leaves or pine needles. She thought she saw a black figure standing next to a tree trunk, but she couldn't tell if it was just a shadow. Was it possible Bobby was following them? Her younger brothers' hollering reached the backyard and reminded Samantha of the time.

Samantha opened the backdoor just as her mother was calling, "Dinner!"

Perfect timing. She was starving. Dinner was homemade pizza tonight with soda, a rare treat in the Taylor house. Samantha scarfed down her food and had barely swallowed her last bite before she asked if she could be excused.

Her mother looked at Samantha, really looked at her, and sighed. She seemed to be thinking "what are we going to do with you?" Samantha broke into the most charming, pleading smile she could manage until her mother broke into a reluctant smile and waved her hand as if to say "Go. Just go."

Samantha pushed her chair back from the table, put her dishes in the sink, and took off up the stairs.

She had research to do on the Spanish settlers from the 1860's. She wanted to see if she could find anything on the brothers named Alfonso and Fernando. What was their last name? That would certainly make things easier. She tried to picture the poem—it was written in the last line.

This is silly—I should bring a notebook and start taking notes on my research. What is Sanz? Suarez? No, it was Saez.

She googled "Alfonso Saez" and "Fernando Saez," but there were too many results. Then she typed in the one phrase of the poem she could remember, *look for Saez, the treasure's within,* and an entire page of relevant articles came up. *Bingo!*

The results were mostly from treasure hunters who gave different interpretations of the poem and who had all failed to find the gold. Some of them looked like they had searched all over the woods trying to decipher the poem. Samantha was a little disheartened. If these grown men with fancy GPS devices and metal detectors hadn't been able to find the treasure, how were she, Ian, and Gerard going to find it?

From what Samantha could tell, only one person even mentioned the mission, but no one appeared to have visited it which meant that no one knew about the second half of the poem. *How had part of the poem gotten into the newspaper? Who had found the journal, but left it there?* And if no one had visited the mission, did that mean no one had read the other journals either? Maybe there was still hope.

She went to bed trying to feel hopeful and sleep overcame her immediately.

12

Samantha woke up with the sun and with excitement rising in her chest. She felt like she was going to burst so she threw the covers off and got dressed. She swallowed her breakfast with minimal chewing, packed her backpack, and went off to meet Ian in record time.

To her surprise, Ian and Sasha were already waiting for her just inside the tree line.

"I could barely sleep last night!" said Ian. "I did some research on the Saez brothers and no one else found the journals."

"I know!" Samantha practically yelled with enthusiasm. "I found the same thing. That one guy mentions the mission."

"But it didn't sound like he visited it," interrupted Ian.

"Yes, exactly!" Samantha fired back. They were walking so fast their feet were barely touching the pine needles and leaves that covered the forest floor.

Sasha could feel the excitement radiating off them and kept jumping or running up ahead. She didn't understand what was going on, but she was happy that everyone else was happy.

When they arrived at the mission, everything was perfectly still and quiet. There was no sign or sound of Gerard. Samantha and Ian stopped and looked at each other with raised eyebrows.

Where was Gerard?

They looked around and didn't see him. Samantha walked to the front door which was standing open and knocked on the rock frame. "Gerard? Hello?" she called out.

"What if he found the treasure and took off without us?" whispered Ian.

"Gerard wouldn't do that," Samantha said laughing. Gerard reminded her of her father in a lot of ways, and her father was a very good man. "Gerard wouldn't be dishonest like that."

She called out again, "Gerard?"

And then they heard a moan coming from the library room. They ran in to find Gerard lifting his head off the desk and yawning. It looked like he had slept there all night. His hair seemed to be fighting with itself and some of the ink had transferred to his cheek.

Ian and Samantha both laughed at him and Sasha greeted him by pushing her head into his hand. Gerard scratched the wolf's head and responded with a sleepy chuckle. He said, "I need a shower."

"But you don't have a shower," said Samantha.

"The waterfall. I use the waterfall as my shower," said Gerard. He stumbled out the front door and seemed to stand more upright as he walked. Sasha stayed behind and settled into the corner for a morning nap.

"Should we wait for him?" asked Ian.

"Nah, he can tell us if he found anything when he gets back," Samantha said. She pulled out the notebook and began to dutifully take notes on her research. She re-wrote the original poem word for word. They dug into their studies with renewed vigor.

About ten minutes later, a wet, clean, and awake Gerard walked into the library.

"I found bupkis last night," said Gerard.

"What's bupkis?" asked Samantha.

Gerard laughed a deep belly laugh. "You know, bupkis. Nothing, zilch, nada. Bupkis!" Gerard was certain he hadn't laughed out loud in years. It felt good.

"Oh," she said. "Bummer. We did some research on the internet, and it doesn't look like anyone has ever found these journals."

"Yeah, only one guy mentions the mission, but it doesn't sound like he even visited it," Ian shared.

"How did you find all of that out?" asked Gerard. "Are the libraries open at night now?"

"Google," they said simultaneously.

"What's Google?"

Ian and Samantha looked at each other. Samantha wasn't sure how to explain Google to a person who had probably never used a modern computer and never experienced the internet.

"It's a thing we use on the computer to find stuff on the internet," said Samantha.

There was an awkward pause where Gerard just looked from Samantha to Ian and back to Samantha again.

"I know what a computer is. They used to carry them around in briefcases when I was in the army. I don't remember kids using them back then though. I guess some things have changed since I've been living out here."

"Probably," said Samantha thoughtfully. She wondered what else changed since Gerard had so definitively turned his back on society. She wondered if the world was as bad as he remembered. Maybe the world had improved since he'd left it.

Samantha was relieved Gerard didn't ask any more questions. One day she would just have to show him the internet and the technology he had missed over the last few decades. She hoped Ian would keep his cell phone tucked away for the time being. She wanted to spend the day researching the past, not trying to explain 'the future' to Gerard.

They turned their attention to the journals and continued their treasure hunt.

Just as Samantha's mind was starting to wander and think about lunch, Ian broke the silence.

"I have something here about a black rock," said Ian. "But it just says that he hit the big black rock while he was digging for a well."

Gerard was so engrossed in dissecting the journal he'd chosen that he wasn't listening to Ian. But the words "black rock" caught his attention.

"Wait, what?" asked Gerard. "Did you say 'black rock'?"

Ian and Samantha both looked at Gerard. "Yeah," said Ian. "Do you know of a big black rock around here?"

Gerard grabbed the book from Ian and read the sentence out loud again. And then he turned back to his own journal, flipping the pages and reading ferociously like he was looking for something specific. "Ah hah!" he said. "Here it is!"

They both looked at Gerard like he was crazy. Even Sasha stirred from her doze and tilted her head at him.

Gerard read from the journal, "*Today, I defeated the rock! Victory is mine. What once impeded my plans now decorates my view and secures my well.*"

"Don't you see?" asked Gerard. "He dug up the rock and then used it to cover his well. All we have to do is find the big black rock that is covering up a well."

"Yeah, but where do we start looking?" asked Ian. "That could be anywhere around here for miles. We'd be searching forever."

Gerard sat down with a disappointed, "Harrumph."

"Well, at least we have one landmark," said Samantha trying to be optimistic.

"Maybe we should take a break and eat lunch," Gerard suggested. He stood, stretched his large frame and scratched his full beard.

They all went outside the walls of the mission where the sky had turned ominous with dark clouds. The weather seemed to fit the mood. They were all disappointed and feeling glum, why shouldn't the sky join them? They ate in thoughtful silence.

Samantha was the first one to feel a raindrop. "It's starting to rain!" she lamented. This treasure hunt was going to be more difficult than she expected. "We'd better start heading home, Ian."

"Maybe we can each take a couple journals home to study," suggested Ian. "If Samantha and I each take two home, then we'd only have a few more to go."

"That's a good idea," said Gerard. "Last year we had a summer rainstorm that lasted an entire week. You could get a lot of reading done in that amount of time." Samantha realized the Saez journals were Gerard's most precious possessions, and he was freely, willingly letting Samantha and Ian borrow them. He was a very generous person, and Samantha was glad he trusted them.

"We promise to take very good care of them," said Samatha. Ian nodded in agreement. They dug out their plastic sandwich bags, turned them inside-out and carefully tucked the journals into the bags to protect the antique books from the rain.

Samantha and Ian headed home, with Sasha leading the way. Ian's usual chattiness was replaced with contemplation and disappointment.

"See you when the rain lets up," called Samantha over her shoulder as she headed to her back door. "Call me if you find anything good."

....

Samantha headed straight to her room and opened up Google. She wanted to find out if there were any distinct-looking rocks in their area that could be seen from satellite photos. She didn't find any obvious ones. But even the big black rock Ian jumped off at the watering hole was covered by trees. The forest was so dense, seeing a rock on a satellite image from Google was unlikely.

She decided to dive into the journals and continue looking for clues. She found a sentence about a hill. It said, *"The rains threaten to wash our camp away. Tomorrow we will head up the hill to secure higher ground."*

She hoped Ian had better luck. She went to sleep dreaming about hills and wells and rain.

When Samantha woke up, she was excited to get back out to the woods, but then she looked out the window. Rain was pouring down outside. She rustled around in her backpack and found the journal she'd been studying.

Diana rolled in her bed and pulled the covers over her head. High schoolers needed a lot of sleep apparently. Instead of dwelling on the rain,

Samantha decided to focus on what she could do—
study.

Her siblings started to wake up and the house
became progressively noisier. Soon there was
yelling and fighting, and then Diana's seemingly
endless phone conversations kept interrupting
Samantha's concentration. *So what if a girl had worn
an orange sweater to the party? Did Diana and her
friend really need to spend so much time worrying
about other people's fashion?* Samantha was
frustrated. She wasn't finding any clues, she was
having trouble concentrating, and the rain just
seemed unfair and ill-timed. She decided to take a
break for breakfast and hoped she would return to
studying with renewed intensity. Samantha was
already back in her room when her mom yelled,
"Samantha! Ian's on the phone!"

Samantha ran downstairs and picked up the
phone.

"Hello?" she said. Samantha was hoping Ian had
good news. She ran back upstairs and closed the
door to her room.

"Hey, it's me," said Ian. "Did you have any luck?"

Wary of Diana's presence in their room,
Samantha made sure Diana was distracted on her
cell phone before she spoke freely to Ian.

"No, not yet," Samantha said. "I found a sentence about a hill, but there wasn't anything terribly noteworthy about it. I put a ribbon in that page to mark it just in case it means something to Gerard. How about you?"

"I found something about a bell, but I can't figure out what this one word is," said Ian. "You want to come over to my house and look at the word? Maybe you'll be able to tell what it is."

Samantha thought this sounded like a great idea! Not only was Ian's house quieter, it also had better snacks. Samantha went downstairs, told her Mom that she was heading to Ian's, and ran down Tolemac Way with the journals. Her backpack was tucked underneath her coat, and she had placed the old journals in brand-new, heavy-duty plastic bags. She didn't want to risk getting even a speck of water on the already fragile books.

Ian opened the door before Samantha had the chance to knock.

"You want something to eat?"

Samantha smiled, "What have you got?"

Ian didn't have restrictions on soda or candy like her family did. He could help himself to anything in the pantry whenever he wanted. He didn't even have to ask before he opened a new package. Samantha stood in front of the pantry and stared. A smorgasbord of cookies, chips, and other snacks stared back at her. Decisions, decisions!

Samantha grabbed her favorites—a candy bar, cheesy chips, and root beer, and they headed up to Ian's room to continue the treasure hunt research.

Ian sat down at his desk where the journal was splayed open and read, *"We heard the bell as we walked on the* something *today signaling another Apache attack."*

Samantha squinted at the faded cursive. She moved the journal until it was directly under the desk lamp. And then she put a blank white piece of paper behind the journal page. Finally, she was able to make out some of the letters. "I think it starts with a 'b' or is that an 'l' and an 'a'. Maybe 'br' or 'lar' ? What could that be?"

"We walked on the *large* today?" asked Ian. "We walked on the *barge* today?"

"No, it's just br, so it'd be 'bradge.' Oh, that must be it, we walked on the bridge today! That makes sense," said Samantha.

"Bridge? Let me see," said Ian. "Yeah, I guess that could be 'bridge'. So there was a bridge!"

"And they could hear the bell from the bridge," said Samantha. "This is a big clue, Ian."

"Yeah, if we can find out where the bridge used to be, then maybe we can find that location," said

Ian with a smile. His smile faded, "But then we still have so many more locations to go!"

Samantha sighed. She felt overwhelmed too. This wasn't going to be easy. It wasn't like they had a treasure map to follow with an 'X' on it. But this wasn't the first time Samantha felt overwhelmed. When she felt overloaded with schoolwork, her parents would say, "How do you eat an elephant? One bite at a time."

Surprisingly their advice usually worked. She learned to break up her seemingly overwhelming projects into smaller tasks and then handled each task one by one.

"Okay," Samantha said. "Let's figure out how many locations we actually have to find. And then whenever we find a clue like this, we can assign it to the correct location. We just need to be methodical and logical and the answers will come."

"Fine, let's try that," said Ian picking up Samantha's notebook with her notes in it. "The second verse of the poem that gives a location is *'Follow the path to the well'* so we know the second location is the well. We know that the well is covered by a big black rock. And the next line says *'Where we listen for the bell'* so we know they could hear the bell from that location.

"And now we know there was also a bridge nearby," said Samantha. "That's a lot of clues! There can't be too many places in the woods with a giant block rock covering a well near a bridge where they could hear a bell ring."

"What bell do you think they could hear ringing in the 1860's? Towns hadn't been built here yet. There were barely any people," said Ian. "Do you think they were referring to the bell at the mission?"

"I think that's definitely a possibility! Great idea," said Samantha. "See? We just need to break it down and take it step by step."

Ian nodded in agreement. "Once we find the well, then all we have to do is find the bear's den, the place the otters used to swim, and then hopefully that will lead us to the creepers, whatever those are."

"Yeah, just four places really," said Samantha. "We can do it."

14

The next day, Samantha woke up to the sun in her eyes, and it took a second for her brain to realize this fact. Once the synapses managed to fire, she jolted out of bed and hurriedly dressed in her now-standard uniform of shorts, a t-shirt, and tennis shoes. She scarfed down breakfast, packed a lunch, grabbed her backpack, and was pleased to see Sasha waiting for her near her old fort. They waited for Ian and then headed north to the abandoned mission.

Gerard was in front of the mission cooking breakfast. Samantha guessed it was a squirrel on a stick - *yum*, she thought sarcastically. Gerard smiled and stood when he saw them. Sasha ran to him and he stroked her head. "I think I know which cave is the bear den!" he said with a big smile.

It hadn't even occurred to Samantha that Gerard's studies may have yielded results. It was a welcome surprise.

"And we found some more clues about the well," said Ian.

"Really?" asked Gerard. "What did you find out?"

Samantha started pulling the ribbon-marked journals from her backpack. "We found out the well is covered by a black rock, it was close to a bridge, and we also suspect that the bell they could hear was the mission bell."

"Hmm… ," said Gerard thoughtfully as he scratched his beard. "It occurred to me that they might be referring to the mission bell, but it just seemed like too much of a coincidence. I only know of one place where there might be a bridge. There is a ravine a few miles northwest of here. It's past the watering hole and borders on bear country which is why I rarely go over there."

He didn't look too excited about the possibility of venturing that far north.

"What about the cave you think might be the old bear den? Is that near it?"

Gerard's eyebrows lifted, "Actually, yeah. The cave I was thinking of *is* near there."

"Well it sounds like we have quite a hike today, we better get going," said Samantha.

"You're right. The only way to know for sure is to see it with our own eyes," said Gerard. He packed up his leftover squirrel, extinguished his fire, and picked up his ragged backpack which had an axe and rope attached to it. The group set out with nervous anticipation. Sasha could sense their excitement and energetically followed them. Ian chatted while they walked, but Samantha and Gerard were both lost in their own thoughts.

Since they were heading north of the mission, the territory was all new for both Ian and Samantha. They both paid extra special attention to their surroundings. Samantha made sure to check her compass periodically so that she knew which direction they were heading and knew which direction would lead her back home. Ian also tied ribbons to small branches as they hiked to mark their trail. They climbed a very steep hill that ended in a plateau covered with grass. Sasha ran up ahead and bound through the tall, wavy grass. Samantha remembered Mr. Turner's lectures and imagined this plateau was similar to the places where buffalo herds used to graze. Of course, no buffalo were here now and only a few deer could be seen off in the distance.

Samantha's legs were very strong from the summer's hiking, but she still welcomed the relief of level ground. Once her breathing returned to a steady pace, Samantha asked Gerard about his discovery.

"Hey Gerard," asked Samantha. "What did you find out in the journals about the bear cave? How did you narrow it down?"

"Oh right," said Gerard. "In one of the journals, Fernando talked about visiting this girl named Lucy. She lived in a large cave that had a giant hole in it. He described the hole in great detail. It was about four feet across, 15-feet deep, and at the bottom of the hole was a rushing river. Well, a few journal entries later, he talked about how scared he was of Lucy and how he wanted her hide for a winter coat. It finally occurred to me that Lucy was actually a bear!"

Ian and Samantha both giggled. Lucy the bear. Samantha hoped the bear and any descendants it may have had were no longer occupying the cave.

"You know of a cave with a big hole?" asked Ian.

"I know I have seen that cave before, but I can't remember exactly where it was," said Gerard. "I am pretty sure it was close to bear country though. Hopefully I'll be able to recognize the terrain once we get close."

They trekked on through the morning over the muddy ground until the sun was almost at its peak. They stopped to eat lunch and guess at how far they had walked. "I bet we've gone at least three miles," said Ian. "We've been walking very fast, and it's been more than two hours."

"I think so too," said Gerard. "We'll be arriving at the ravine and finding the bridge before you know it!"

And a few minutes later, they did just that. Samantha saw the edge of the forest first and ran to the ledge. She looked down a 40-foot ravine that spanned 15 feet across. It wasn't very wide at all, but the ravine stretched north and south as far as she could see. She felt queasy as her fear of heights made her stomach flip flop.

She took a step back and tried to think about whether or not this was the correct spot. If the Saez brothers wanted to get from one side to the other, they would have had to build a bridge.

"Careful!" yelled Ian. He ran up beside Samantha. "Whoa!"

Gerard came up behind them and looked at the ravine. "It's been a long time since I've come this way. The last time I was here, it must have been monsoon season because there was water rushing down the ravine." Now there was only a trickle of water about a foot across at the bottom of the ravine.

"Should we start looking for where the old bridge might have been?" asked Samantha. She had already looked north and south down the ravine. So far, they saw no sign of a bridge. Any bridge that may have been here before was definitely no longer intact.

Gerard looked north and then he looked south, "I feel like Lucy's old cave might be this way." He pointed to the north.

They all moved together along the west side of the ravine and kept their eyes peeled for remnants of a bridge. "We should look for any part of the old bridge like rope or an old wooden post," said Ian. "But we should also look for a safe way to climb down into the ravine. If the bridge is gone, we won't have any way to get across."

About ten minutes later, Ian exclaimed, "Hey, look! Could that be part of a bridge?" He pointed across the ravine to a few strands of rope hanging down from the east side of the ledge.

Samantha immediately started looking for where the bridge might have connected on their side–the west side. A few feet from the ledge, just inside the tree line, she saw a wooden pole about four feet tall sticking out of the ground. "Here's where the bridge ended on our side!" she exclaimed.

Gerard and Ian hurried to the pole. A frayed piece of rope was still hanging from a hole in the wooden post. "Now what?" Samantha asked.

They had found the bridge which was supposed to be near the well, but there was no way to get across the ravine where the bear cave was probably located.

"I have an idea," said Gerard. "What if we cut down a tree and use it as a bridge? The ravine is only about 15 feet across so we wouldn't even need to find a very big tree."

"What about finding a way to climb down into the ravine?" said Ian. "Maybe there is a place where it's safe enough for us to climb down and then up to the other side."

"But that could take a long time," Gerard said. "I can have a tree chopped down in less than an hour. Finding a safe place to climb into the ravine could take all day."

"Why don't we do both?" suggested Samantha. She didn't like the idea of crossing the ravine over a narrow tree trunk. "Gerard, you can chop down the tree while Ian and I spend one hour trying to find a safe place to cross."

Gerard nodded in agreement and set off to find a tree that was more than 20 feet tall and had a thick enough trunk. Sasha chose to stay with Gerard and dutifully followed him in his search.

Samantha and Ian continued north in search of a safe place to cross. About 20 minutes into their hike, Samantha saw what looked like giant stairs on the east wall of the ledge. Ian saw them too and stopped. They both peered over the west side of the ledge and saw that their side had the giant stairs too.

"With my fear of heights, I don't know if I can do this," said Samantha.

Ian was already carefully dropping himself onto the first step. "Come on, it's not too bad. Look, it's like a platform. There is a lot of room to stand."

Samantha cautiously peered over the side and saw Ian standing on a two-foot platform. It looked like someone had carved the rock to be flat. It was definitely man-made. The platform Ian was standing on gently sloped down and Ian was able to step down to the next platform which sloped in the opposite direction. He went back and forth from platform to platform until he was on the ravine floor. "See! That was easy!" He looked up and waited for Samantha.

She slowly moved onto the first platform and then carefully lowered herself down to the next platform. When she finally made it to the ravine floor, she looked up and then she looked at Ian with wide eyes, "I did it! I made it the entire way without falling!"

They hopped over the small stream of water and started up the other side. Samantha climbed more confidently this time, but wasn't ready to even glance down while she was climbing. They back-tracked along the east ridge until they were opposite from where Gerard was cutting down the tree.

"Gerard!" yelled Ian. "We found some steps and made it across!"

Gerard stopped mid-axe-swing and looked across the ravine at Ian and Samantha.

"Okay. I'm almost done here."

He was slightly disappointed that the middle schoolers' solution had yielded a faster result, but he knew a tree trunk bridge would save them time on the way back.

The trunk now had a wedge-shaped chunk missing from its side. Gerard kept swinging the axe and with each powerful stroke, the wound in the tree grew larger. A loud crack resonated through the ravine when the trunk broke, then a whoosh filled their ears as the branches sailed through the air. Ian and Samantha scurried out of the way to avoid getting hit by the falling tree's branches. The tree made a loud thud as it landed in place.

As soon as the tree came to its resting position, Ian turned to Samantha and said disappointedly, "We forgot to yell timber!" Samantha laughed at him.

Gerard pushed the tree trunk closer to the edge to center it over the dangerous ravine. He straddled the trunk and chopped off branches as he deftly moved along the trunk. Sasha followed closely behind him and didn't seem to have any trouble balancing on the trunk even though it wasn't very wide. By the time they joined Ian and Samantha, the wood was mostly smooth on the top. Branches still hung from the sides and bottom. It probably wouldn't pass an official safety inspection, but it was an adequate bridge.

Now they needed to find the well or the bear's cave. The east side of the ridge sloped down into a valley where there were more bushes than trees. Gerard thought the valley was a prime place to look for a well, so they formed a line and looked for the big black rock Fernando Saez had described in his journal so many years ago.

After about a half hour of combing the valley, Samantha saw a large, black, flat rock. She yelled and then tried to move it. It was too heavy and didn't budge. Gerard tried to move it, and couldn't at first because nature had secured the rock's position over the years. It was held in place by stubborn weeds and compacted dirt.

"We should have brought a shovel or something," said Ian.

"Yeah, we need a lever of some kind," said Gerard. "Do you see any long branches or sticks we could use?"

Ian and Samantha both shook their heads.

"I guess we should head toward the trees and look for one," said Samantha as she pointed to the forest at the edge of the grassy valley. They walked through the knee-high grass together and split up when they reached the trees.

Ian found a branch first, but Gerard thought it looked rotted and would break too easily. Samantha found the next branch, but they all agreed it was too thin. Sasha thought they were playing a game and started carrying branches back to Gerard to inspect. They all laughed at her enthusiasm and cleverness.

Finally, Gerard found the ideal lever for their task. Ian and Samantha offered to help carry it, but Gerard said it was easier to just drag the branch on his own.

When they reached the black rock, Gerard shoved the thinnest end of the branch as far under the rock as he could. They needed to put weight on the thicker end of the branch so Ian and Samantha both grabbed the branch, tucked in their knees, and hung in place like monkeys. The branch and rock both stayed securely in place.

Gerard laughed at how silly they looked hanging there. Then he took hold of the high end of the branch and yanked down. The branch held its form and didn't splinter or break.

Finally the rock moved! And once Gerard displaced it, he easily rocked it back and forth out of the way. Samantha and Ian scurried around Gerard to get a glimpse of what was underneath the rock.

At first Samantha just saw long weeds flopping over and filling the spot where the rock used to be. And then she saw blackness—the ominous opening of the well. Samantha walked on the weeds close to the opening to get a better look, and suddenly her feet fell through the weeds. There was no ground beneath them—they had only been camouflaging the hole.

As she fell, time seemed to slow down and her thoughts sped up. The panicked feeling caused her stomach to wrench and she thought back to the time she'd fallen from the high dive. She remembered what it felt like to struggle to breathe. She remembered the pressure on her lungs. Her voice was momentarily strangled while she dreaded the fear and pain that waited for her at the bottom of the well.

Suddenly, her reflexes took over and she grasped for anything she could hang on to. Her right hand managed to find a weed and some dirt on the well's edge to grab. The stubborn weed root slowed her fall for a second, but it wasn't enough to hold her. Sasha let out a short but very loud *bark* as Samantha fell into the darkness. Her piercing screams reverberated off the walls of the well.

15

The fall ended with a splash as Samantha's feet found the pool at the bottom of the well. The water was deeper than Samantha was tall and she was submerged into the dark, frigid water. Her reflexes took over once again, and she struggled to the top of the water to fill her lungs with air. She was too busy gasping to continue screaming. Her whole body was shivering and shaking as she tread water.

"Samantha!!! Samantha are you okay," Ian yelled as his face appeared over the opening of the well. "Are you hurt?" His voice was full of concern and fear.

"I'm okay," she managed to say in between gasps. "At least I think I am." She heard the hysteria creeping into her voice. *Not now. Now is not the time to start freaking out.*

More thoughts about her high dive "accident" seeped into Samantha's mind, and she worked hard to keep control of herself.

Gerard's face was over the well now too. "Samantha, it's okay. Everything's going to be fine. The most important thing is to remain calm, okay? Do you understand?"

His voice was like her dad's. It was smooth, calm, and didn't demand, but assumed obedience. Gerard had likely been in much worse situations in the army. Rescuing Samantha from a well would hardly be a challenge for a strong, experienced man like Gerard, right? Gerard paused, waiting for Samantha's answer.

"Okay," Samantha said as she forced herself to breathe. *Everything is going to be okay. Gerard and Ian are here. All they have to do is throw down a rope and I'll be rescued.* She remembered seeing a coiled rope on Gerard's backpack this morning and hoped it would be long enough.

Gerard continued, "Are you hurt?"

"I don't think so."

"Are you able to touch the bottom?"

"No, I'm treading water. It's too deep. It's really dark down here," Samantha's voice started to falter.

Gerard was already working on detaching his rope from his backpack as he said, "Samantha, I need you to do something for me. Can you take a big, long breath in through your nose? And let it out slowly through your mouth?"

"I'll try."

Samantha was breathing hard from the cold and the adrenaline, but she managed to inhale through her nose and exhale through her mouth.

"Good," said Gerard. "Now keep doing that. Try counting to four as you breathe in and count to four as you breathe out." He was busy tying the rope around his waist.

Samantha figured she must be at least fifteen feet from the surface. It was a deep well. And it was dark. The thought occurred to her that she might not be the only living thing swimming in this well. Bugs, mold, snakes… She pushed the scary thoughts from her mind and focused on the positive. She was able to tread water, she couldn't feel any injuries, and Ian and Gerard were here to save her.

The rope flopped down the wall of the well and landed on the water next to Samantha. Gerard's face re-appeared over the opening. "Samantha, I need you to tie the rope around yourself. Can you do that?"

Samantha's now blue lips were chattering, but she managed to say yes loud enough for Gerard to hear her. She had never been quite so grateful for the Girl Scouts. Samantha knew how to tie a bowline knot which is a good secure knot that could be used to carry a person's weight in a rope rescue mission like this one. Even with cold fingers and chattering teeth she was able to tread water with her legs and fasten the rope securely under her arms.

"I'm ready," she yelled in between chatters. Gerard gave the rope a tug to test its strength, and then he started pulling the rope slowly and steadily. Samantha's body rose out of the water, and she pressed her feet and hands against the wall to steady her ascent. The rope was tight around her chest and very uncomfortable. It hindered her arm movements, but she continued to reach out to the well wall for support. She could hear Sasha whimpering and letting out an occasional worried yelp as she ascended up the well shaft. The slow climb up the wall seemed to take forever, but soon enough, her head was in the sunlight. Next her shoulders emerged from the well opening, and then she felt Gerard's strength as he gripped her under her shoulders and pulled her onto solid, dry ground.

Gerard immediately gave her a big bear hug. He had tears in his eyes and said, "You are a brave, brave girl Samantha."

The thought of losing Samantha was too much for Gerard. All of the feelings of loss, all of the nightmares were welling up. He felt overwhelmed, like the years of sadness were bubbling up and could erupt any moment. He set Samantha gingerly on the grass and then walked away. He shook his head and willed the memories to stay buried. He forced them back behind the mental walls he had built years ago.

With tears in his eyes, Ian gave Samantha his much smaller version of a bear hug. *More of a bear cub hug*, she thought. She squeezed him back. Sasha apparently felt left out and nosed her way into the hug. Samantha scratched her ears.

"Don't ever do that again!" Ian exclaimed. "That was scary! I thought you were a goner for sure."

"Yeah, it was," Samantha agreed as she laughed at Ian's dramatic response. "But I knew you guys would get me out." Her fear and dread were replaced with an almost giddy relief.

The afternoon sun felt so good! She could feel the freezing cold water evaporating from her skin. Samantha assessed herself. She still had two arms and two legs. She looked and made sure that she had all of her fingers. Ankles were intact, knees were scraped, and she was covered in mud, but she was alive and she was okay. Gratitude overwhelmed her.

"Ian, I didn't even panic!" said Samantha with pride in her voice. "And I finally got to use my bowline knot."

She held up the knot that was still tied around her. She was proud of herself for not breaking down and staying calm under pressure.

Ian inspected it and was impressed. She looked at Gerard to show him the knot as he was wiping away a tear. He walked back to them and looked at the knot.

"Impressive, indeed. Where did you learn how to do that?" Gerard asked.

"Girl Scouts. Are you okay Gerard?" Samantha forgot about her own trauma and focused her concern on Gerard. He seemed to be more affected than she was.

"Yeah, you just remind me of this girl I used to know…and lost," said Gerard quietly. "It brought back some bad memories."

Samantha didn't know what to say so she just hugged him. "I'm okay. I'm fine. Thank you for saving me." She looked up at him and Gerard managed to smile back at her. He rubbed the top of her head.

Gerard spoke up, "Well that certainly was a close call!"

He went to push the big rock back into place. Ian helped too and the black rock was soon back where they had found it. The well would remain closed and safe to passersby now.

"Well, I think we've all had enough treasure hunting for one day. We'd better start heading back," Gerard said.

Ian and Samantha didn't argue with Gerard's wise decision. Ian chatted as they walked pointing out different birds that he knew and reminding them all to be careful about snakes. But Samantha was worried about Gerard. *What girl had he lost? And was losing the girl the real reason he moved to the woods all those years ago?*

Samantha thought about how lucky she was to have Gerard and Ian there to help her after she fell. If only Ian had been there, she may have been stuck in the well for a long time. She likely would have had to tread water for hours in the dark well while Ian ran for help. Who knows what could have happened? She realized Gerard had saved her life. She made a promise to herself to never forget, and to look for opportunities to help him in the future.

As she reflected on her fall, she realized she had been brave. Sure, she screamed on the way down, but then she treaded water, didn't freak out, and managed to remember her knot-tying skills. It was a terrifying situation, and anyone would have been scared. But she stayed calm and was rescued immediately. She felt very grateful to have such wonderful friends.

When they arrived at the fallen log that traversed the ravine, Samantha hesitated before she ventured out onto the bridge. The trunk was wide enough to crawl on, and it carried Gerard's weight easily. Normally she would have thought about all the bad things that could happen, but after the well incident today, she crawled out on the trunk with her new-found bravery. It was odd, but she felt confident now. If she could stay calm and survive falling down a well, then crawling on a tree trunk to get over a ravine seemed easy all of a sudden.

After a long hike back, Samantha, Ian, and Sasha left Gerard at the mission and made their own way home. It was earlier than usual when Samantha reached her backyard. She hugged Ian one more time before they parted ways, "I don't know what I would have done without you and Gerard. You are both true friends."

"Thanks, Samantha," said Ian. "You're a good friend too." He smiled one of the smiles that lit up his whole face.

She felt tears pooling in her eyes again so she turned away, took a deep breath, and then headed to her house. She took off her mud-caked shoes before she went inside and silently climbed the stairs. She took a long, hot shower. Samantha scraped off the biggest pieces of mud and shoved the clothes deep into the laundry basket. With any luck they would be tossed into the washing machine without scrutiny. *Diana would definitely freak out if she knew my muddy clothes were mixed in with her fancy outfits.*

Meanwhile at the mission, Gerard built a fire and watched it as tears streamed down his cheeks. Almost losing Samantha today tore down the walls he had so carefully erected years ago. No amount of will power could hold back the wave of memories and the painful anguish he had felt on that fateful night.

Many years ago, Gerard was deliriously happy. He had it all including a wife, a daughter, and a budding career in the military. His wife was his partner, truly his better half. She was no stranger to deployments and raising a child almost entirely by herself. She knew these were her duties as a military wife—and she rose to the challenge. He couldn't remember ever hearing her complain. And his smart, beautiful daughter adored him. They were so lucky.

One Friday night, while he was finishing up paperwork for work, his wife and daughter got a hankering for ice cream. The girls agreed to go out and pick it up and then they would all watch a movie together. Gerard had a lot of work to do and he focused all of his attention on it until the doorbell rang. He looked at the clock and saw it was almost eight o'clock. *Who could be ringing the doorbell this late?* He didn't remember when the girls left, but it seemed like they should be back any time now.

On the other side of the peephole, a police officer with a notebook stood waiting for Gerard to open the door. Conjectures about the officer's presence reeled in Gerard's mind. *Was there a criminal loose in the neighborhood? Had a crime been committed*? He opened the door, looked at the young officer's face, and then he knew.

At that moment, Gerard knew his life was over.

"Gerard Harris?" the officer asked. Gerard managed to nod his head. He held his breath as the officer continued, "I am sorry to disturb you at this hour, but I need to… Can we sit down?"

Gerard nodded silently and followed the officer to the living room. Gerard sat at the edge of a chair and with an ashen face, he silently begged the officer to not say what he was undoubtedly about to say.

"I'm sorry to be the one to inform you, but your wife and daughter have been in a car accident," the officer said, clearly distressed. "They were hit by a semi-truck that had a tire blow out. It lost control and… they didn't make it." He almost whispered the last part, but the words sounded like they had been yelled through a bullhorn directly into Gerard's ears. Even now, the words pounded in his head.

The officer took a deep breath and continued as professionally as possible. He went on to inform Gerard about the accident and started asking him routine questions. Gerard didn't hear any of it. He fell to his knees and sobbed.

Over the next few months Gerard became apathetic about everything in his life. His military career seemed unimportant, his friends' sympathies became a burden, and he fell into a deep depression. As soon as he was able, he left the military and sold the house filled with joyful memories. His life was over. He grew fearful of what he would become if he didn't get away. He needed to start a new life—another life where nothing could remind him of what he'd lost. And he needed to find peace, a deep peace that could only be found in nature.

Six months after he lost his family, Gerard moved to the woods and started his second life.

16

The next day, the three treasure hunters and the wolf met at the old mission once again. The wolf was chasing a rabbit around the mission while the three humans were regrouping and trying to come up with a plan.

"We found the location from the second verse yesterday," said Samantha. "The well where they could hear the mission bell ringing. Should we go back there and look for clues? Or should we try to find another location?"

"The first verse in the poem is *'Pass our friend who hibernates, be quiet and sly don't tempt the fates,'*" said Ian. "Gerard, did anything look familiar to you yesterday? You said you remembered seeing a cave with a big hole just like the journal said."

"There was one thing that looked kind of familiar yesterday. I remember this unique formation in the mountain with the cave. It looks kind of like elephant ears, and the cave with the big hole is right in the middle of the ears. I can't be sure, but I think I may have seen that formation yesterday from the valley where we found the well."

The hike to the tree bridge seemed shorter today and their anticipation urged them to move more quickly. Soon they were at the ravine and crossed the bridge to arrive at the valley with the well. Gerard looked at the mountain to the north—it was so tall the top was still white with snow.

Gerard pointed, "Do you see the elephant ears? There's the left one, and there's the right one. And I think I see the sharp rock that hangs over the cliff. It's a little whiter than the rocks around it."

Samantha saw what Gerard was pointing at. "That's a long way up," she said. "We'd better get started."

They hiked in a straight line up the mountain and then stumbled onto a path with switchbacks. It was lunch time when they reached the rock that Gerard thought might be the cave, but no one wanted to stop to eat—they were too curious.

As they approached the white rock, Gerard announced, "It is a cave! I was right. Let's see if this is the cave that Fernando described in his journal." Ian pulled out a flashlight and moved toward the entrance of the cave.

"Let me go first," said Gerard, taking the flashlight from Ian. "I'm sure no bears live here anymore, but just in case, you both stay out here." He wasn't taking any chances—he wasn't going to lose anyone today. Sasha followed Gerard into the cave cautiously.

After what seemed like an eternity, Gerard and Sasha emerged from the cave. "It's the one," he said with a satisfied grin. Despite his best efforts, Gerard was getting excited about this treasure hunt. He had given up on it years ago, but now he was starting to feel hopeful. And more importantly, he was enjoying himself. He hadn't gone on a real adventure in a long time, and he hadn't had friends in a *very* long time.

Ian and Samantha scrambled to follow Gerard into the cave. "You have to be extremely careful," he said. "There is a giant hole, and the floor is slippery from being wet. There are also bats, but most of them are asleep right now."

Samantha immediately slowed down as she did not want to repeat the accident from yesterday. She also felt some trepidation at the thought of bats flying around.

Ian slowed down too. Ian, like most boys, thought danger and adventure should go together hand-in-hand, but he was scared when Samantha fell down the well yesterday. He wasn't going to risk anything going wrong today. He did secretly hope that he would get to see a bat though. He knew they were dangerous if they bit you because they carried lots of diseases, but he just wanted to see one.

As they moved deeper into the cave, the sound of running water intensified. They approached the hole carefully and saw the rushing river below. It splashed them, and the cool water in the cool cave was a welcome relief after the hot hike in the Arizona sun. They paused for a moment to enjoy the mist.

Ian shined his flashlight around the cave and saw a plethora of bats covering the walls and ceiling. The bats were all sleeping until Ian said, "Whoa!" too loudly. Some of the bats woke up and started darting around the cave in abrupt flying patterns. Their high-pitched screeches filled the cave. Sasha got scared and barked which caused even more bats to join in the chaos. Sasha immediately took off for the entrance of the cave.

Samantha instinctively covered her head with her arms even though she only felt the wind from the bats wings, not the bats themselves. Not a single bat ran into her or touched her skin. She remembered learning about how bats use sonar and echolocation sounds to "see," and despite her acute anxiety, she was impressed at their ability to fly so quickly and accurately.

Every bone in Samantha's body wanted to start moving toward the entrance to the cave, but the floor was wet and slippery, and she couldn't see very well because the air was thick with bats now. She didn't let her fear take over. She forced herself to take a breath and remain still while she figured out what to do next. Ian reacted impulsively though and bumped into Samantha. She used to wall to steady herself.

"Careful," said Gerard as he took hold of Ian's shoulder. Gerard's strong hand reassured Ian and he was able to calm himself down. Gerard instructed Ian to hold onto Samantha's shoulder so they formed a human chain. Samantha led them slowly and carefully away from the hole. She kept one hand on the wall and used her other arm to shield her face from the bats. Once they were away from the slippery, wet floor Samantha walked faster and then they all ran the remaining few yards toward the sunlight.

The treasure hunters exited the cave with a cloud of bats flying out behind them. Sasha was a safe distance from the cave, pacing. She barked when she saw her friends.

"That was so cool!" yelled Ian as he watched the dark cloud fly up, around, and back into the cave.

"You did a good job staying calm, Samantha," said Gerard. "And you led us out of the cave so carefully. I'm really proud of you." Gerard gave Samantha a side hug and patted her shoulder.

Samantha was proud of herself too. She had reacted well to the bat emergency and kept her wits through the stressful ordeal.

"Yeah, Samantha you were cool as a cucumber," said Ian. "Sorry I bumped into you. I got scared at first."

"That's okay," said Samantha. "I'm just glad we all got out safely. Did any of the bats actually touch you?"

"No!" said Ian. "That was the coolest part! I felt the wind from their wings, but I never actually felt any bats."

"Yeah, me either," said Gerard. "Well, I don't know about you two, but I am starving." Samantha and Ian nodded vigorously. They pulled out their lunches and ate hungrily. Gerard shared his lunch with Sasha.

"We have found two clues now," reported Samantha.

"Does it help us, though?" asked Ian. "We know where the bear den was and we know where the well was. But what we really need to find are the creepers from the last verse in the poem. And we're not any closer to finding those."

"Yes, we are," said Gerard. "Now that we have two clues, we know what direction the clues are going in, and that is going to help us narrow down our search quite a bit."

"You're absolutely right," said Samantha as she looked at her notebook. "They started at the bear den, then they headed to the well. Now we know where both of those places are, and we know they were traveling south. Then they headed to the otters and then the creepers where the treasure is."

"We still have no idea where the otters and creepers are though," said Ian with a sigh.

"Yeah, you're right," said Samantha. They had studied, searched, hiked, and tried so hard, but weren't close to finding the treasure at all. It was discouraging.

"What are we going to do with the treasure when we find it?" Ian asked, changing the subject.

Samantha and Gerard both laughed. "*If* we find the treasure, I think we should give it to a museum," said Gerard.

"What?!" both Samantha and Ian exclaimed in unison.

Ian continued, "You mean we're doing all of this work and won't even get to keep any of it?"

"Well, I don't know. I've never found a treasure before. Maybe they'll give you a finder's fee or something," said Gerard. "And if that doesn't work out, then you could always write a book about our little adventure here and sell that."

He chuckled at their disappointment in not becoming instantly rich.

"I was going to buy this drone I've been wanting," said Ian disappointedly.

"Do you still want to keep looking for the treasure?" asked Gerard. Looking at their glum faces, he now felt a little sorry for them. "We don't have to keep going. You're right, this is a lot of work and it's dangerous. If you don't want to keep treasure hunting, then we can stop."

"No!" cried Samantha. "I want to keep looking." She hadn't had this much fun ever! And she wasn't sure what she'd do with all of that money anyway. She thought she could use some of it for college even though she was planning on getting scholarships for her good grades.

Ian didn't look as certain. Samantha challenged him, "What were you going to do with all of that money anyway? Your parents buy you everything you want as it is."

Ian shook his head at her. "That's not true. I've been wanting the Millennium Falcon LEGO set for years, for as long as I can remember, and they won't get it for me. And there are a lot of other cool things I would buy too."

"Well, do you want to stop?" asked Samantha.

Ian sighed, "No, I don't want to stop. You're right. This is too much fun."

They started walking down the mountain. "I'm bummed we might not get to keep the money though. Whatever happened to finders keepers?"

Ian lamented the entire way back to the mission about the toys he'd planned on buying and how unfair it was they wouldn't get to keep the gold. Gerard seemed amused and Samantha genuinely felt a little sorry for Ian.

17

· ·

Samantha woke up in a sweat, not because she'd had a bad dream, but because it was just plain hot. Her parents were too thrifty with the air conditioner in her opinion. When Samantha or one of her siblings complained, her parents would sweetly suggest they could start controlling the air conditioner once they started paying the bill.

Last summer Diana had mischievously turned down the temperature on the air conditioner without permission, and their dad noticed within minutes. It was like he had air-conditioning radar. Diana was grounded for a whole week for "being dishonest."

Samantha felt stumped with their treasure hunt, and the heat wasn't exactly a motivator. She wanted to take a day off, and all she could think about was finding some relief from the heat. *Too bad we don't have a pool. Wait a minute… I know what we can do today!*

She called Ian's cell phone, and Ian's voice came on the line, "Holy cow, it's hot today!"

Samantha heard a door close, presumably Ian's bedroom door.

"Do you want to go to the swimming hole?" Ian asked.

"Yes! That's what I was thinking too! I could use a day off of treasure hunting." Samantha was relieved Ian agreed. She wasn't sure she could handle another stressful adventure in the woods. She needed a break.

They met up close to Samantha's fort and walked the distance to the swimming hole with the waterfall. Sasha wasn't there to greet them this morning, and they guessed she needed a day off too. They'd both brought lots of water and were dressed in swimsuits this time. The air felt cooler as they approached the water and both of them jumped right into the still icy water.

"This is amazing!" yelled Samantha as she surfaced and giggled.

Ian was already swimming toward the edge. She watched him get out and start climbing the rocks on the north side of the pool. They looked slippery and some of the rocks jutted out over the water like a diving board.

"Watch this!" Ian was standing on one of the rocks that stuck out over the water. It was only a few feet high, and the water below was clear. They could see all the way to the bottom which looked at least a dozen feet deep. He tucked his legs up into a cannonball and was rewarded with a big splash.

Once Samantha wiped the water from her eyes, and stopped laughing, a thought popped in her head. *That looked like fun.*

And she realized it did look like a lot of fun. This was the summer of courage and being brave. She didn't want to miss out on fun anymore. She didn't want her fear to control so many of her choices. Samantha's facial expression became resolute. "I'm going to try it," she said.

"What? Miss I'm-afraid-of-heights is going to jump from all the way up there?!" Ian asked in a taunting manner. Ian knew it was barely higher than a diving board and that Samantha could easily make the jump.

Samantha smirked at him and then swam to the edge. She got out of the swimming hole and stepped over the slippery rocks carefully. She reached the rock and walked toward the edge. Flashbacks of the high dive and her recent fall into the well appeared in her mind, and she struggled to push them away. There was no Bobby here today. She could take her time and jump when she was ready.

She closed her eyes and took a deep breath. She willed her heart to stop racing and her body to calm down. Then with a quiet confidence, she opened her eyes, took the final step to the edge of the rock, and jumped. She kept a rigid pencil form the entire way down with her arms pressed against her sides and her toes pointed, reaching for the water. Her hair blew upwards as she sucked in one last breath before she hit the water.

The icy cold liquid enveloped her from toe to head in an instant, and it was a thrill. Her downward trajectory stopped before her feet touched the rocks on the bottom, and she started moving upward. She was laughing when she surfaced, laughing with relief and with pride. How much fun had she missed because of fear?

They both got out of the icy water and took turns jumping from the "diving board" for the next hour. When they were pruny and their lips were blue, they sat on the large, sun-warmed rocks to eat lunch.

Simultaneously, Ian and Samantha turned toward the west to see what had caused a rustling sound in the bushes. Sasha exploded from the tree line and ran to greet them with many kisses. Gerard was close behind her and was carrying some wiry contraptions over his shoulder. They looked like squirrel traps. Thankfully they were empty, and didn't have any animals in them yet.

Samantha realized they had forgotten to tell Gerard about their day off of treasure hunting. He could have been waiting for them this morning, and she felt her actions were rude. She immediately said, "I'm sorry we didn't tell you we weren't up for hiking today. We should have gone to the mission first to let you know."

"Oh, that's okay! I figured it was too hot for treasure hunting today," said Gerard. "I see you've made a rather good choice and decided to swim instead. I need to go reset my traps anyway. I've been neglecting my chores."

"Do you want some help?" Ian asked hopefully.

"Sure!" said Gerard. "I've got about five more of these to set, and then I'm all done for the day."

"You want to come too, Samantha?" Ian asked.

"I think I'm going to stay and swim," she said. Sasha sat next to her, and Samantha stroked her head.

Ian put away the remains of his lunch, slipped on his clothes and shoes, and they walked toward the east. Samantha lay back on the warm rock and tucked an arm under her head. Sasha lay down next to her with a contented sigh. The warmth of the sun and her full belly coaxed Samantha to sleep. She and Sasha napped until Samantha woke up abruptly to the sound of Sasha growling. It was her low, threatening growl accompanied by a defensive stance and bared teeth. Samantha was once again reminded that Sasha was still a wolf, and a wild one at that.

Sasha was ready to attack. Samantha quickly sat up and looked around. She didn't see anyone in any direction. Sasha's growling stopped, and she relaxed her position. Samantha let out a breath, and then she heard distant footsteps running away from the northwest side of the swimming hole. The hurried movements crushed dry leaves and disturbed pine needles.

Having done her job, Sasha lay back down and closed her eyes. Samantha wasn't ready to relax quite yet though. *Who was that? Who was following them? Did someone know they were treasure hunting?* The only way another person could have found out about their treasure hunt was if someone was spying on them. Samantha didn't like that one bit.

Samantha knew animals had superior senses of smell and hearing so she felt safe with Sasha as her bodyguard. Whoever was in the woods surely wouldn't come back while Sasha was standing guard. Samantha let out a sigh—she had hoped for a day off to relax, and now another mystery was nagging at her.

A drop of sweat rolled down Samantha's forehead, and she realized how hot and uncomfortable she was. She started walking toward the pool and then came up with an idea. She didn't want today to be ruined by whoever was in the woods. She decided to distract herself with a challenge—a height challenge. She was going to jump off of progressively higher rocks until she was able to jump off the highest one.

Samantha started out small. She jumped from the safety of a rock that was a few feet higher than the "diving board." And then she did it again until she got bored and pushed herself to a taller ledge closer to the waterfall. *Don't look down. Just do it. Courage is doing something even when you're afraid.* She knew it was a safe jump. She knew the water was deep enough, but still she stood.

"I'm going to jump," she reported to Sasha who had resumed her nap in the sun and was unfazed by Samantha's announcement. Samantha took a deep breath and jumped. She meant to scream, but the sound caught in her throat. The water hit her bottom hard with a slap and then she was deep under water. And she was fine. She resurfaced without incident. Instead of a scream emerging from her lips, laughter came out. She was pretty sure her completely ungraceful jump into the water must have looked funny. And besides the momentary slap of pain, it was fun!

Without pausing for too long, Samantha went to the same taller ledge and jumped again. It was even more fun the second time! She kept on going.

Not long after Samantha accomplished this mini-victory over her fear of heights, Gerard and Ian came back from their walk.

Before Samantha could tell them everything that happened while they were away, Ian exclaimed, "We saw a bear track; it was huge!"

"I thought there weren't bears in this part of the woods," Samantha said.

"I bet it was just a lone bear that strayed too far from home," said Gerard.

"Well, that's still scary," said Samantha.

"We set up all the squirrel traps, and I even set one up all by myself," bragged Ian.

Gerard asked, "Did anything happen while we were gone?"

"Actually, yeah," replied Samantha, now a bit more serious. "A little while ago, Sasha started growling at something in the woods, and then I heard footsteps running away from over there." She pointed to the northwest. "I was nervous, but I knew I was safe with Sasha."

Samantha decided to keep her other news a secret. Maybe one day she'd surprise them and jump from the highest rock.

"Hmmm…. ," said Gerard as he started walking the northwestern perimeter of the watering hole presumably looking for tracks or other evidence. Ian followed him, and Gerard started showing him what he saw—broken branches, a squashed berry, and then footprints. They were made by someone who had bigger feet than Ian, but much smaller feet than Gerard.

Ian said, "I bet it was that Bobby Lustin."

Gerard didn't reply as he started following the tracks. Samantha put on her clothes and hurried to catch up to them. She was curious to see where the trail would lead. Gerard showed them where to step in order to avoid messing up the footprints. Since pine needles and leaves covered a lot of the forest floor, they only saw partial footprints once every couple of steps. It was tedious business. Sasha seemed to know just where to walk to avoid messing up the footprints. How she understood what they were doing, Samantha didn't know.

The trail veered to the north and they continued to track the footprints for a while. Sasha trotted ahead sniffing the air and following her nose. Samantha stopped to scrutinize a broken branch and realized she had leaves sticking to her shoe. "Ugh, I stepped in gum!" she exclaimed.

Ian and Gerard both returned to her side. "Is it the bright green stuff?" asked Ian.

"Of course it is," said Samantha in disgust as she used a stick to remove the gooeyness. "Yuck."

Sasha started barking suddenly, and Gerard was the first one at her side. "It's a snake," said Gerard.

He backed up and said, "Sasha, come here."

Ian and Samantha scurried to see the snake but only saw the last few tan rattles slip into the bush. Gerard was petting Sasha's head, trying to calm her down.

"Good girl. Good girl. But it's gone now. You don't need to be afraid anymore," he said in a consoling tone. She was still whining and fidgety.

Samantha heard the unmistakable buzz of wasps. "Maybe she's afraid of the wasps too," she conjectured.

They looked up and saw a large, perfectly shaped paper wasp nest hanging from a branch far above them. Samantha was admiring the wasps' ability to build such a robust home, when she noticed that the hive wasn't the only thing hanging out in the tree.

18

· ·

Bobby Lustin was positioned on a tree branch directly above the wasp hive. He was intently watching them, presumably spying on them. He must have heard them talking about the treasure or something, Samantha surmised. She was furious.

"Bobby Lustin, what are you doing?" she yelled up at him. She was impressed at the weight of her voice. She would have never confronted a Lustin a few months ago.

Bobby sheepishly stuttered, "I just wanted to see what you were doing. I wasn't spying or anything, I just… I…. it kind of looked like you were having fun."

Samantha was surprised by his answer. "You thought it looked like we were having fun? Are you sure you aren't spying on us?"

"I swear I'm not," Bobby said in a high indignant voice. "I haven't even told my brothers about the treasure or anything!" As soon as he said it, Bobby realized he shouldn't have admitted he knew about the treasure. Now they would never believe he hadn't been spying on them all summer. He just wanted to join their summer adventure. All of their hiking, swimming, and treasure hunting looked like a lot of fun. He had been following them sometimes, ever since they caught him accidentally starting the fire.

When Bobby saw that Gerard was friends with Ian, Samantha, and the wolf, he had gotten curious. Gerard wasn't the scary old man Bobby thought he was. Gerard actually seemed pretty cool and knew a lot of stuff about the woods. Bobby sighed and fidgeted as he adjusted his position on the tree branch. He didn't know what to say to make them believe he wasn't ill-intentioned.

Suddenly, there was a loud crack, and Bobby screamed. The branch snapped, and he fell with it. The full weight of Bobby and the branch knocked the wasp hive loose from the branch below. He flailed violently to find something to hang on to. He caught a small branch that stopped his descent. The hive fell and exploded as it hit the ground. A cloud of very angry wasps enveloped them.

Without hesitation, Gerard yelled *"Run!"* and shoved the middle schoolers toward the south, back the way they had come. Ian, Sasha, and Samantha ran quickly, but it wasn't fast enough to outrun the wasps. The angry buzzers swarmed around them and harassed them from head to toe.

Gerard stayed and watched as Bobby's small branch broke. He fell the final ten feet to the forest floor and landed on his butt with a thud. Gerard moved to help Bobby up and said "Come on, we have to run to the watering hole."

But Bobby was scared, certain they would accuse him of trying to steal the treasure, and took off to the west toward his house. Gerard considered following Bobby for a second, but then the wasps became so thick, he could barely see. He turned to follow Ian and Samantha.

Ian yelled something, but Samantha couldn't hear him over the buzzing and the thudding of her own heartbeat. Her vision was obscured by the wasps too, but she could see Ian ahead of her. Samantha felt a wasp sting on her arm and cried out in pain. She stopped in alarm, and the wasp swarm thickened.

She felt Ian grab her upper arm and pull her along. She started moving again. "Keep running," Ian pleaded. Another wasp stung her left thigh. She didn't stop this time. Or the next.

Within a minute or two of sprinting down the path, they came to a cliff. It was the north side of the watering hole, the top of the waterfall. Samantha was terrified. *Now what are we going to do?* The wasp swarm was only getting thicker.

Gerard finally caught up to them, and saw they were both hesitating. He leaned down to Samantha's eye level and said, "We have to jump."

Samantha's stomach dropped and she started shaking her head.

"We have to get in the water," said Gerard. He already had wasp stings on his face. As Samantha looked into Gerard's fearful eyes, she finally and fully understood the gravity of the danger surrounding them. Her stomach flipped and then she became resolute. She had to do this. She had to get into the water.

Ian heard Gerard and yelled, "Come on, Samantha!" Ian grabbed her hand and pulled her to the edge. He turned to her and said sincerely, "You can do this. I'll jump with you."

Samantha was too overwhelmed with fear to think. Ian sounded so sure, and she knew she had to trust him. She nodded her head, bent her knees, and they both jumped off the steep cliff together.

On the way down, Samantha felt the air rushing around her driving the wasps away. The buzzing noise was replaced by the soothing sound of water cascading all around them. Time seemed to stop for a moment, and she felt a kind of clarity she'd never experienced before. It was like someone hit the reset button on her brain. She felt every moment intensely as they fell through the air. Samantha looked left to see Ian having less fun than he usually did jumping from tall rocks into water. She consciously unlinked her hand from Ian's and moved her hands to her side, just like she had practiced. She prepared for splashdown with a newfound sense of confidence and calmness.

Her feet hit the water first, and the rest of her body followed. The momentum took her deep into the watering hole. She didn't open her eyes, because she knew it'd be black all around her. Her lungs felt restricted under the pressure, but she didn't panic, and she didn't struggle. She calmly waited for the descent to end, and then she started kicking as hard as she could, driving herself up toward the surface. She dared to open her eyes and saw the light above her, shimmering and sliding around in the column of water still above her head. The sunshine seemed far away, but Samantha didn't let that observation affect her determination. Her only goal was to kick harder. The light grew closer. And then she broke through the surface gasping for air.

Ian grabbed her hand and started pulling her to the side. "We have to get out of the way for Gerard!" he yelled over the noisy waterfall.

Samantha started swimming toward the edge and within a second, Gerard's body was falling through the air. Something didn't look right. Gerard wasn't forming a pencil or a cannonball. He was tilting to the side as he fell. He tried to regain control at the last second, but he hit the water on his left side. The clap his body made against the water sounded painful.

Samantha yelled, "No!" and started swimming to where Gerard had hit the water. Ian swam with her too. Gerard's head rose above the surface, and he gasped for air. When he'd filled his lungs with oxygen, Gerard said, "Ow! That wasn't fun."

Samantha asked "Are you okay?" She saw that he had red spots from the wasp stings on his face. He must have been stung several more times while he was waiting for Samantha and Ian to swim to safety.

"Yeah, I'm okay," grunted Gerard. He reached the edge and pulled himself out. He started picking the stingers out of his skin.

"We need to get you to a hospital," said Ian.

Gerard just shook his head, "No, I'll be fine." And he managed a tired smile. He continued to pull out stingers from his arms, his chest, his legs.

"Do you want us to pull the stingers out of your back?" Ian asked. He nodded. Ian and Samantha quickly got out of the water to the rock where Gerard was sitting and started carefully plucking out the stingers. When they finished, Gerard sunk back into the cool water hoping it would help with the pain and swelling. Ian and Samantha didn't bother to shed their wet clothes and joined him. They both watched Gerard with concern.

Breaking the silence, Samantha asked, "Hey, where's Sasha?"

They all started looking around. At the sound of her name, Sasha howled. The noise seemed to come from up above. Samantha looked up but didn't see her. She called, "Sasha!" and they heard the wolf whine.

Ian got out of the pool and started climbing the slippery rocks next to the waterfall. "What if she's hurt?" Ian asked.

At the thought, Samantha hopped out of the pool and started climbing the cliff wall along with Ian. Samantha cooed at Sasha hoping to keep her calm and climbed as fast as she could while still being safe. She used the vines that hung on either side of the waterfall to steady her ascent. About halfway up the waterfall, they knew Sasha was near because the whines grew louder.

"Where is she?" asked Ian, who was now a few feet below Samantha.

Samantha found a small platform where she could stand on her tiptoes and steadied herself with one of the sturdier vines that hung down from up above. She poked her head through the rushing waterfall and tried to see where Sasha was hiding. What she found took her breath away.

19

Samantha was too stunned to speak or even move. Water was still spraying around her face and her first thought was *I must not be seeing things clearly.* Sasha wasn't injured, but she was anxious. She was pacing on flat ground in what looked like the mouth of a cave. The hole behind the waterfall was about four feet wide and four feet tall. The entrance was tall enough for even a grown man to crawl into it.

Ian looked up and watched what appeared to be a magic trick. Samantha lifted herself up and disappeared in the waterfall. It looked like the waterfall had just absorbed her. He quickly climbed the rest of the way and stuck his head carefully through the water. He too disappeared through the waterfall into the cave.

Samantha was sitting against one of the walls and rhythmically petting Sasha, trying to calm her. Ian yelled something, but it was too loud to hear each other over the waterfall and the echos reverberating off the cave walls. Sasha's anxiety overtook her and she moved into the blackness beyond them. Samantha yelled after her, but Sasha didn't reappear. She looked at Ian and mouthed, "What now?"

He pointed to the black depths of the cave and shrugged. Her eyes widened in hesitation, but then she shrugged too. Today really couldn't be any more terrifying. They had survived a cloud of angry wasps, a near death-defying jump off a cliff, and now they were following a wolf into a dark cave. Just another day in what was now Samantha's adventurous life. They crawled on their hands and knees slowly. Samantha touched something slimy. She shrieked reflexively but brushed it off her hand and then she kept going.

The cave was pitch black now. They were completely dependent on their hands to feel things around them. Samantha would periodically reach out in front of her to make sure she didn't bump her head. As they crawled slowly through the cave, the din of the water subsided. They had moved about ten feet when Samantha's hand touched Sasha's wet furry coat. She found her head and scratched behind her ears and under her chin. As Samantha's hand moved around Sasha's head, her wrist brushed against something hard. *Was one of Sasha's teeth sticking out?*

"What is this?" Samantha asked Sasha. It was quieter now, further back in the cave away from the waterfall.

"What is what? I can't see anything," complained Ian.

Samantha investigated by touch and discovered Sasha was carrying something hard and rough in her mouth. Sasha let go of the object, and Samantha felt it. It felt heavy like a rock.

"Sasha had something in her mouth. Here, see if you can tell what it is."

She blindly searched for Ian and then placed the object in his hand so he could feel it too.

"Let's go back toward the light," Ian suggested.

Samantha and Sasha followed him back to the mouth of the cave. A thought occurred to Samantha that the rock could be gold, but she laughed off the idea. This couldn't be the famous Saez treasure. There weren't any creepers around here, and there wasn't any frozen water either. What were the odds that they could have found a 150-year-old treasure by accident?

Ian was crawling faster now. They reached the mouth of the cave where the sun's rays could pierce the waterfall.

Ian opened his fist, and they both looked at a large gold nugget. It wasn't rusty even though it was wet. Ian turned it over, stared at it in disbelief and handed it to Samantha. *Could this be part of the treasure they'd been searching for all summer? What if they actually found it?*

"We need to get a better look," Ian yelled over the din of rushing water.

"And show Gerard," Samantha yelled back excitedly.

Ian stuffed the possible gold in his pocket, stuck his head through the waterfall and then jumped. Sasha whined and paced at the mouth of the cave. She was too nervous to jump.

Samantha pet her and said, "Sasha, you have to jump. You have to. There isn't any other way down."

Samantha was so excited to see the nugget in better light that she was losing patience with the wolf who was also apparently afraid of heights. Samantha knew what she had to do. She started pushing Sasha toward the edge. It was only about ten feet down. Sasha would be fine. Sasha resisted at first, but then she very clumsily fell down the waterfall. She hit the water with a yelp, resurfaced, and started swimming to shore. She clambered onto the rock where Ian was and shook her mane with full force.

Samantha jumped with a gleeful shout—jumping off of things was fun. She was glad she wouldn't be missing out because of fear anymore. She was excited to get a better look at the gold and show Gerard. She reached Ian and Sasha quickly.

Ian and Samantha both started calling for Gerard. He wasn't yelling back at them—something was wrong. They both looked at each other with equally worried expressions. Then they heard a grunt and Sasha sprinted to where Gerard was leaning up against a rock about ten yards away. He was slumped over and his chin was practically resting on his chest. Samantha reached him first and took his face in both her hands. She carefully lifted his head and a disfigured, swollen face stared back at her. Even the skin under his beard was red and swollen. The wasps seemed to have stung him everywhere. He was mumbling something, but she couldn't make out the words.

Sasha was whining and pacing again. And then realizing that she couldn't do anything, she laid down and gingerly placed her head on Gerard's leg. He raised his hand and painfully placed it on her head.

Ian exclaimed "We need to get help! We have to go right now!"

20

Samantha was crying now, and she lowered Gerard's head carefully. She patted him softly on the shoulder, "We're going to go get help, Gerard. Sasha, you stay." Sasha raised her eyebrows at the sound of her name and stayed in place.

The man who had saved Samantha's life now needed her help. She vividly remembered the silent promise she'd made to look for opportunities to help Gerard. This was it. This was her chance to repay him for saving her when she fell down the well.

It broke Samantha's heart to leave Gerard, but she knew she couldn't help him here. Samantha and Ian raced out of the watering hole. They were yelling plans at each other as they ran.

"I'm going to tell my dad to get medication for wasp stings," yelled Ian.

"I'm going to tell my dad to come help too," Samantha managed between sobs. "We might need to carry him to where an ambulance can pick him up." Tears were streaming down her face. Her vision was clouded by her salty tears, and she tripped on a root. She went sprawling face first onto the dirty forest floor.

Ian came back to help her up. He wiped her tears away and said, "It's going to be okay. Our parents are going to help us."

Samantha nodded and wiped more tears away. Ian gave her a hug. And then he said, "Come on. We have to go."

Samantha hadn't even bothered to assess her injuries from the fall, but she could feel warm blood running down her left shin. She must have skinned her knee pretty badly.

They reached Samantha's house first, and Ian said, "I'll meet you back here in five minutes."

Samantha agreed and sprinted to her back door. She yanked the sliding door open and yelled, "Dad! Dad!" Her voice was sheer panic.

She heard her father's footsteps coming from his office, and he said, "What? Samantha, what is it?"

Roger halted in fright as he saw his baby girl covered in mud with blood running down her leg. Her messy wet hair was full of leaves. She looked like she'd gotten into a fight with the forest. He pulled a blanket from the pile and closed the distance between them. He put the blanket over her shoulders and gave her a hug.

"Samantha, are you okay?" her dad asked sweetly and calmly.

At this point, the rest of her family had trickled into the room to see what all the ruckus was about. Samantha rarely caused a commotion so her family members were shocked at her appearance and her obvious distress.

Samantha was sobbing and trying to tell her dad that Gerard needed help. She started pushing him away, but he hugged her harder. Then Samantha grew determined. She stopped sobbing, pushed her dad away, and in the most mature voice she had ever heard come out of her own mouth, she said, "My friend is injured in the forest and needs your help."

She spoke with such authority the room fell silent. Even James and William understood something serious was happening.

Roger's arms fell to his side along with the blanket, and he said, "What happened?" in a grave tone.

"Ian and I made friends with an old man who lives in the woods. He was stung by a bunch of wasps and now he is all swollen and can't move. We need to get him to a hospital."

Samantha's mother became concerned, "What do you mean you made friends with an old man? If he's a grown man, why can't he take care of himself?" Her incessant questions were ignored by both Samantha and her dad.

Samantha's dad looked into Samantha's eyes, put his hands on her shoulders and nodded. Roger made the decision to help. "I'll get the big wagon we used to cart around James and William when they were younger." He headed for the garage.

"Ian's dad is getting medicine, but I'll get some water and blankets," Samantha called after him and then headed toward the kitchen with her mother in tow.

"Samantha Grace," her mother almost yelled at her. "Answer me this instant. What old man are you talking about?" Diana and Jack were poised in the doorway, not wanting to miss out on the drama. James and William were back to the den playing with their LEGO sets.

Samantha didn't stop gathering the necessities, and she tried to think of what else they would need. "Gerard is my friend, Mom. He saved my life once and now he needs our help."

"Saved your life?" Samantha's mom nearly hit the ceiling. "Why was your life in danger? What is going on?"

Roger came into the kitchen and placed his hands on his wife's shoulders. "Love, we need to stay calm right now," he said in a slow, even tone. "You're right, we're going to get all of these questions answered, but getting worked up right now isn't going to help the situation."

He turned to Samantha, "Young lady, when this emergency is handled, we are going to have a nice, long chat." Samantha swallowed hard and then nodded.

Her mother guffawed and blustered, and then conceded with a nod. Roger hugged her, and she capitulated into his arms.

Roger looked at Samantha, "Are you ready? Let's go." They ran for the back door.

***

Ian started calling for his dad as soon as his house was in view. He could see BBQ smoke coming from their backyard, and he hoped they were outside. His mom was lounging in the hot tub, and his dad was tending to the burgers on the grill.

"Ian, you're just in time for burgers," his dad said in a jolly tone.

"Dad! You need to grab your medical bag. There is someone hurt in the woods, and we can't move him," Ian managed to say while panting.

"What's wrong? What happened?" his dad asked.

"A wasp nest fell, and he got stung a lot. And now he's delirious and swollen and can't move," Ian spewed out the facts in haste. He tried to remember any other details that could be medically relevant.

Ian's dad turned and ran into the house. He took the Hippocratic oath seriously even if his typical patients usually had four legs. Ian's mom was silent at first and then she asked with tears welling up in her eyes, "Is Samantha okay?"

"Yeah, yeah Samantha is fine," said Ian. He followed his dad into the house hoping to move him along. His dad already had on shoes and his medical bag in his hand.

Ian rushed him out the door, and they met Samantha and her dad at the tree line behind Samantha's house. Ian and Samantha took off at a trot with both dads behind them.

No one said a word the entire way to the watering hole. The wind in the trees and the hard breathing from the four rescuers was deafening. Samantha was sure they jogged for hours before they reached the watering hole.

Gerard and Sasha were right where Samantha and Ian had left them. Sasha still had her head on Gerard's leg. Roger and Ian's dad both stopped in their tracks and stared at the wolf.

"Come here, Samantha," Roger said as he started backing away slowly. He was afraid of what the large wolf might do, especially since the wolf seemed to have claimed the injured man. Roger wanted to help, but not if it meant risking his daughter's life.

"Dad, it's Sasha. She's our friend," Samantha continued walking toward Gerard and showed both dads how sweet Sasha was. The adults approached the injured man cautiously and Sasha reluctantly moved away to give them room to work. Ian pet the wolf and reassured her everything would be okay as he watched his dad kneel down next to Gerard.

Ian's dad lifted Gerard's head and started yelling, "Can you hear me?"

He turned to Ian, "Do you know his name?"

"Gerard!" Samantha and Ian said in unison.

"Gerard, can you hear me?" Ian's dad was rubbing Gerard's chest in an effort to help him regain consciousness.

Gerard mumbled deliriously just as he had before. "He has too many stings," Ian's dad reported. "The venom induced a toxic reaction. Do you know if he's allergic to any medication?" Ian and Samantha both shrugged helplessly.

"Gerard!" Ian's dad practically yelled at him. "I need you to take these pills, okay?" He placed the two white pills in Gerard's mouth, gave him a sip of water from the bottle Samantha had grabbed. Some water dribbled out of Gerard's mouth, but then he managed to swallow.

"We need to get him to a hospital," Ian's dad informed them. Samantha wheeled the wagon as close to Gerard as possible, and the dads lifted him onto the blankets and pillows. It took all four of them to roll Gerard out of the watering hole area. The dads pulled while Ian and Samantha pushed. Sasha whined and dutifully stayed by the wagon's side. Once they were out of the steep uphill portion, the dads took turns jogging as they pulled the wagon. Ian and Samantha jogged behind them.

When Ian's dad took over pulling the wagon, Roger jogged with his daughter. "You and I are going to have a nice long talk," he said ominously. He looked at her as if he was looking at a brand-new person—as though he'd have to get to know Samantha all over again.

Samantha swallowed hard again and realized that she did have a lot to explain to her parents. She figured she would be in big trouble, but her dad, as always, would at least be understanding.

Ian knew where his phone started getting cell service, and he called 911 as soon as he could.

"Have them meet us in front of the Taylors' house," Ian's dad said. Ian explained the situation as best as he could. When they asked for more details about Gerard, Ian realized he couldn't answer any of them. He didn't know Gerard's age, his last name, or any other relevant details. What Ian did know was that Gerard was a good man and needed help immediately.

As they reached the Taylor house, Sasha hung back in the tree line to pace and whine. Somehow, she understood she needed to wait for Gerard in the woods.

The ambulance was already there when they arrived. Thankfully Samantha's siblings had been instructed by their mother to stay in the house. Her mom and the rest of the clan watched from the side windows with curiosity and concern. Ian, Samantha, and their dads were exhausted from running almost non-stop for miles through the woods. Ian's dad started explaining the situation in medical terms to the paramedics as they loaded Gerard onto a gurney.

Samantha tried to follow the gurney straight into the back of the ambulance, but was stopped by the seemingly impenetrable arm of a third paramedic. After a hurried but stern conversation between her dad and the paramedic, Samantha found herself climbing back into the ambulance, with her dad right behind her. There wasn't room for Ian and his dad.

"We'll follow you in our car," Ian said.

Samantha held Gerard's hand the entire way to the hospital while she cried silently. The paramedics pricked his arm and inserted an IV. They took his blood pressure, hooked him up to several machines, and even gave him a shot of some kind. When the shot took effect, Gerard woke up sucking air. He almost started to sit up, but the chest strap held him down.

"What happened?" He asked in bewilderment. "Where am I?" He was wild-eyed as he tried to gather his wits.

"Gerard, it's okay," Samantha said. "We're taking you to the hospital. You were stung by the wasps, remember? I'm going to stay with you, and my dad is here too."

Gerard struggled to focus on her dad's face and managed to say, "Roger?" before he passed out.

21

. . . .

"Gerry?" her dad asked incredulously.

Receiving no reply from the injured man, Roger leaned back on the uncomfortable bench seat feeling a mixture of disbelief and concern. The paramedics continued to attend to the ailing patient. *Gerard Harris?* Roger nearly said aloud.

"Do you know him, Dad?" Samantha asked through her tears.

"It's hard to tell from the swelling, but I think this might be Gerard Harris. He's the one I told you stories about–Hairy Gerry."

"Really?" asked Samantha. She had always thought Gerry was spelled with a "J." It had never occurred to her that Gerard might go by the nickname "Gerry."

"How can that be?" Samantha asked.

"Well, Gerry lost his family–his wife and his daughter–in a bad semi-truck accident many years ago. He left the military, he stopped answering his phone, and just disappeared. None of us knew where he went."

"Huh," said Samantha. "One time, he said I reminded him of a girl he used to know."

"Yeah, his daughter was about your age when she passed away," Roger said. "Wow, he's been living in the woods this entire time?"

"I guess so. He lives in an abandoned mission in the forest," Samantha replied. They sat through the rest of the short ambulance ride in silence.

At the hospital, Gerard was wheeled through double doors where only medical personnel and patients were allowed. Samantha and her dad were instructed to wait outside. They took the opportunity to address Samantha's muddy and bleeding leg. She cleaned it as well as she could and then they found seats in the waiting room.

Ian and his dad soon joined them. Once they were all settled, Samantha's dad said, "Okay, what have you two been doing this summer? I think now is a good time to share the whole story."

Ian and Samantha looked sheepish as they shifted in their seats. Samantha took a deep breath and said, "Well, it all started one Friday when I decided to walk home through the woods after school. Then the next day I found Sasha. She was just a puppy back then, and she was injured."

Samantha told them how Ian helped her save the Mexican gray wolf. She paused and waited for her father to scold her, but he didn't. Both of their dads sat patiently and listened to every word of their summer adventures.

Ian told them about the army blanket and then they reluctantly told their fathers about the treasure hunt. Through an unspoken bond, they both failed to mention anything about the cave in the waterfall, or the fact that Ian still had a gold nugget in his pocket. They did explain the whole fiasco about Bobby Lustin, his fire, and the wasps. It was an accident. He hadn't maliciously dropped a horde of angry wasps on them. It had just happened, and Gerard was in the hospital because he had chosen to save their lives. He had graciously chosen to jump last and suffered the consequences.

The dads listened in awe. At various parts in the story they shook their heads, looked surprised, or took deep breaths. But they didn't speak except to ask questions a couple of times. They listened patiently, and at the end of the story Roger said, "I'm glad you're both okay. We'll have to talk about what to do with you two later." He hugged his daughter.

As they waited, Samantha ended up falling asleep on her dad's arm. Long after night had fallen, she woke up when a doctor came out to tell them Gerard was stable but in a coma. All four of them decided to head home and return to the hospital in the morning.

During the first day of Gerard's coma, Samantha's parents had a long talk with her. Samantha had to explain what she had been doing all summer and why she hadn't told her parents about the treasure hunt, the well, the bats, or the fire. She tried to explain how safe she felt because Gerard and Sasha were always there to protect her. She also told them about overcoming her fear of heights and how she had bravely handled many situations in the forest. She told them about saving Sasha and standing up to bullies. She tried to make them understand how much more mature she was now because of her new friends and the challenges she'd overcome.

They listened and asked a lot of questions. In the end, they were mostly upset that Samantha had kept her adventures a secret. They reassured her that they loved her and wanted to know what was happening in her life, even if it was scary. Samantha was allowed to keep her friends and continue to hike in the woods, but she had to report what happened to her parents each night. Samantha eagerly agreed.

22

· ·

Gerard squinted at the sunshine beaming through the hospital room window until two young faces filled his frame of vision. "Hey," whispered Gerard in a husky voice. He smiled and tried to sit up.

"It's okay. Don't sit up," said Samantha. "I'll raise the bed." She found the button.

"We've been reading to you while you were in your coma," said Ian. "Do you remember any of Robinson Crusoe?"

Gerard tried to laugh, but his throat was too dry. He reached for the pink, plastic water jug and poured himself a cup.

"How long have I been out?" Gerard asked, still disoriented.

"You've been in a coma for three days," said Samantha. "The doctors said you might still be able to hear us even though you were unconscious so we read to you as much as we could." They had spent every day by Gerard's side faithfully reading to him, holding his hand, and talking to him.

Gerard scratched his head as a memory resurfaced. "Did I see Roger? Or was that just a dream?"

"Yeah, Roger is my dad," said Samantha. "He didn't recognize you at first because of all the wasp stings, but he figured it out. He's been telling me stories about you for years, and he calls you 'Hairy Gerry.'" Samantha giggled.

Gerard laughed heartily. "That's right! The guys in the Army used to call me that—I had forgotten. Well I'll be glad to catch up with him and reminisce about the good old days.

"So I was out for three whole days? What else did I miss?" Gerard asked.

Ian and Samantha looked at each other and smiled knowingly.

Gerard noticed their sly glance and asked, "What's going on, you two?" His voice was returning.

Samantha looked to see if anyone was close enough to hear the secret she was about to share. "Gerard, we found the treasure."

Ian started reaching into his pocket to pull out the nugget. Gerard's eyebrows raised, "You found it?" he asked.

"We found it," said Samantha. "You, Sasha, Ian, and me. We all found it together."

"What do you mean? Where was it?" Gerard asked.

Ian and Samantha both started talking at the same time and laughed, but Ian let Samantha tell it.

"Well after Bobby Lustin knocked down the wasp nest, we all ran to the cliff above the watering hole. Bobby felt bad by the way. He and his mom visited you in the hospital and gave you those flowers." Samantha pointed to a vase with a small cluster of white daisies.

"Anyway, you guys convinced me to jump with Ian. And then you followed a few seconds later." Samantha wasn't sure what Gerard remembered after his traumatic day, so she recounted all the key points.

"Well, Sasha was apparently too afraid to jump so she skidded down the cliff a ways and ended up landing in a cave behind the waterfall. We couldn't see Sasha, but we followed the sound of her whines. The waterfall completely covers the cave so you can't see it unless you stick your head through the water. After we took your stingers out, we went to look for Sasha and found her in the cave. It was loud and dark, but Sasha walked to the back of the cave so we followed her. And then it was too dark to see, but I felt a hard, metallic thing in her mouth."

At this point, Ian pulled the gold nugget out of his pocket and slyly passed it to Gerard. Gerard turned to his side so his back was to the hallway, providing cover for their secret. He couldn't believe his eyes. It looked like real gold. It wasn't rusted or tarnished. At first glance it looked genuine.

"Did you tell anyone about this? Have you had it inspected?" Gerard asked.

"No, we wanted to wait for you to come with us to see if the rest of it is there," said Ian. "We wanted to make sure you were there for the official discovery. But we're pretty sure it's the Saez treasure. We pieced together some of the clues from the poem."

"Yeah, we think the 'creepers' in the poem refer to the long vines that hang next to the waterfall," said Samantha.

"And do you know if the watering hole freezes in the winter time?" asked Ian. "We thought maybe the water froze and that's why the poem says 'walk on water'."

"The watering hole sometimes gets clumps of ice in the winter, but it's never frozen solid," said Gerard. "And the waterfall runs year round now. Maybe back then it didn't."

"Huh, well we never found out where the otters used to live either," said Samantha. "I guess some things will just have to remain a mystery."

"We need to go get a better look at that cave," said Gerard. He was still skeptical, but he laughed wryly, "I may have been showering under the treasure for all these years."

"I know!" exclaimed Samantha. "It was right under our noses the entire time."

"You need to hurry up and get better so that we can get out to the watering hole," said Ian.

Gerard laid back on his soft pillow, "I don't know. I haven't slept in a real bed for years. This is feeling pretty good right now." He pretended to sleep and made them laugh.

Exactly one day later, Gerard was discharged from the hospital. Samantha, Ian, and Roger came to pick him up. The two army buddies had caught up the day before and spent some time reminiscing about the good old days.

The nurse wheeled Gerard's wheelchair to the curb where the car was waiting. Gerard stood up and stretched.

"Gerry, good to see you up and around," Roger said as he shook Gerard's hand and then gave him a hug. Gerard didn't look any worse for the wear except for a few lingering red marks on his face. The doctors told him he'd make a complete recovery, and his health wasn't in danger. They contributed his quick healing to how healthy and fit he was.

When they reached Samantha's house, Gerard, Samantha, and Ian immediately headed for the woods to find Sasha. "Hey, be careful!" Roger shouted after them.

Gerard was certain Sasha was fine, but Samantha was worried Sasha would get scared or run away without them around. Sasha wasn't at the tree line so Gerard whistled as loud as he could. Within a minute they heard Sasha galloping through the bushes. She jumped on Gerard and almost knocked him over. She was whining, licking him, and clearly overwhelmed with joy. She just couldn't contain herself. And then she greeted Samantha and Ian with the same enthusiasm but with less jumping.

Samantha and Ian went into the Taylor house to quickly round up some supplies, and then the four of them headed into the forest with a singular focus.

Samantha was the first one to remove her shoes when they reached the watering hole. She put on a small backpack that carried a flashlight and a small garden shovel which were both in sealed plastic bags. She started climbing the rock wall. Ian started climbing the other side and they raced to see who could reach the cave first. They couldn't remember exactly how high up the cave was and had to keep ducking their heads under the waterfall to check. Ian reached the cave first and disappeared into the waterfall.

Gerard watched from below as he was a little nervous about exerting himself too soon after the accident. "Well, I'll be…" he muttered.

It looked like Ian had melted into the water, and then Samantha performed the same magic trick a second later. Gerard stroked Sasha's head and waited.

The cave somehow looked even darker than before. Giddy with excitement, they both unwrapped their flashlights and turned them on. The ceiling of the cave rose quickly. After crawling about four feet, Samantha and Ian were able to stand up and walk. Ian shouted, and the echo reverberated against the walls. Samantha's giggles were swallowed by the deafening sound of the waterfall.

They walked down a sort of hallway and then the walls receded and gave way to a large room. To Samantha's surprise, the room looked empty. "Where is it?" she asked.

Ian was surprised too. "I guess we have to just look around. It has to be here somewhere."

Samantha turned to the right and started moving along the wall looking for holes, cracks, or crevices where the gold might be. Ian did the same thing along the left wall.

Samantha looked up and down. She felt along the wall, and tried to think of places where she would hide gold if it was up to her. She pointed the flashlight from the floor to the wall and back again. She thought she saw a glimmer and pointed her flashlight directly at it. The glimmer was coming through a crack in the ground.

"Ian!" Samantha yelled. "Ian come here!" She put her flashlight down and started moving rocks as fast as she could. She pulled out her garden shovel and started removing dirt too. Ian rushed over and together they started shoveling. Samantha suddenly realized that anything they uncovered would likely be of historical significance.

"Ian, we have to be careful as we dig," said Samantha. "Anything buried here might be important." They set aside their shovels and started using their hands to brush away dirt. Soon enough they uncovered the top of a disintegrating burlap sack with gold nuggets inside.

"We found it!!!!" Ian yelled.

"We found it!!!" yelled Samantha.

"You found it?" asked Gerard. He was standing at the entrance to the room with a flashlight in hand.

"I was too curious! I couldn't wait any longer."

He quickly walked to the treasure where Samantha and Ian hugged him. "Hey look," he said as he aimed his flashlight at the wall. Right above the buried gold, the word 'Saez' had been hurriedly carved into the wall.

"We found it," Samantha whispered as she inspected the gold in her hand. "We really found it." She jumped up and down and then twirled. Ian was running in circles at this point yelling, "We're rich! We're all gonna be rich!"

Gerard carefully chose a gold nugget from the bag and held it in his hand. He smiled silently, and a tear rolled down his cheek. He felt full of gratitude and hope for the first time in many years.

23

It was Friday afternoon, and the first week of school had just ended. Samantha and Ian left class and headed for the woods where Sasha and Gerard greeted them for their afternoon hike to Samantha's house. When they reached Samantha's backyard, Ian headed left toward his house while Gerard and Sasha headed right. They all had to get ready for the party at the local museum tonight. The Saez treasure was going to be displayed for the first time.

Since the gold had been abandoned on public land and no one could claim to be the rightful owner, the authorities weren't sure what to do with the gold. Lawyers and historians were called, and they cited Treasure Trove law which dictated that Gerard, Samantha, and Ian were now the rightful owners of the gold. Of course they didn't actually want to keep the gold pieces, so a museum in New York had agreed to buy them.

Tonight the New York museum was hosting a party at the local museum and displaying the gold for the first time in the city where it was found. In a few months, the exhibit would move to the main museum in New York.

Their successful Saez treasure hunt had received a lot of local press, and their story even appeared in some national publications. Each article was accompanied by a photo of the treasure hunters and the wolf standing next to the waterfall with the sacks of gold in front of them. Gerard, Ian, and Samantha were all happy and standing proud in the photo. Even Sasha looked a little more regal than usual in the picture.

The museum party would be well-attended not only because of the gold and its historical significance, but also because the New York museum would be announcing the worth of the gold. Tonight, the three treasure hunters would find out exactly how much money they'd receive.

Samantha had already asked her parents to set up a college fund for her. She planned on giving a portion to her parents and her siblings as well. Ian's parents were going to let him spend some of it on toys, but the rest would go into a trust for when he was older.

When Gerard was discharged from the hospital, he went back to live in the mission, but it didn't feel right to him. When his wife and daughter had died, he started his second life in the woods, but that life seemed needlessly empty now. He knew he had money in his old investment accounts, and the money had been growing for many years. He decided to use some of the savings to buy a house at the end of Tolemac Way where he could be close to the woods, Samantha, and Ian. Sasha visited Gerard often, and they kept each other company. Gerard told Samantha and Ian he was going to start his third life now. He was looking into becoming a consultant for the military or writing a book. He also thought traveling the world sounded like fun.

Later that evening, Samantha and Ian walked into the museum and saw the Saez treasure exhibit right away. The large glass enclosure was well lit and stood in the center of the main room. Archeologists and historians had gathered additional artifacts and added them to the exhibit including an old map of the forest and a sketch of the mission when it was new. They extracted the part of the cave wall that read 'Saez,' and it sat propped on a podium next to the journals and the newspaper clipping. The burlap sacks had been salvaged and were a prominent feature of the exhibit. They were bulging with sparkling gold and were carefully arranged to show off the treasure. The large photo of the treasure hunters and Sasha at the waterfall sat on an easel. Samantha felt a little thrill every time she looked at the photo.

Samantha and Ian chatted with their classmates while Gerard was introduced to friends of their parents. Bobby Lustin attended the party with his mom and he was able to apologize to Gerard about the wasps in person.

Gerard gave Bobby his full attention and said, "I know you didn't knock down the nest on purpose. It was an accident. I'm just glad you're okay, kid." Gerard patted him on the shoulder.

Bobby looked relieved at first and then he remembered the fire he'd accidentally started. He hadn't gotten in trouble for that so he figured Gerard, Samantha, and Ian must have realized he didn't start it on purpose. Bobby spoke up again, "I'm really sorry about the other thing too. Thanks for letting people know that was an accident too." He turned red and hung his head in embarrassment.

Gerard looked at Bobby's worn out clothes and his worn out mother, and realized that Bobby probably had a pretty hard life. Gerard sensed earnestness in the young boy's apology and decided to respond with generosity.

"Hey, we all deserve a second chance, right?" Gerard said. He wanted to tell Bobby to use his second chance wisely and to not squander it. He wanted to shake the boy and tell him to respect the forest and to respect the people around him. Most of all, he wanted to encourage Bobby to make better decisions so that he could respect himself.

Instead, Gerard patted him on the shoulder, and said, "You're going to grow up to be a good man, Bobby Lustin."

Bobby looked up and smiled at the tall, strong man. Gerard hoped Bobby would remember his words and at least try to live up to them.

The museum curator from New York walked to the podium at the front of the room and started the presentation for the evening. Samantha, Ian, and Gerard were asked to join him on stage. Gerard had trimmed, but not shaved his beard. He was dressed in a charcoal suit and looked very handsome. Ian was wearing a trendy blue suit that complemented his tan skin, and Samantha had chosen a pale pink dress for the occasion.

The curator told the story about the Saez brothers and the poem to the packed room. Then he congratulated the trio on their bravery and tenacity during the dangerous treasure hunt. The crowd responded with applause.

Samantha was bursting with pride as she heard their story being told out loud. Something about the way her name sounded through the speakers was so... *adventurous*. They had indeed shown tenacity, and she had overcome many of her fears. Her thoughts started drifting to what their next adventure might be. Would they go on another treasure hunt? Solve another mystery? She caught herself and brought her attention back to the present moment. She didn't want to miss a second of tonight's party.

She looked out at her family and her classmates, the people who used to know her well. Now, no one except Ian and Gerard understood the transformation she had undergone. Samantha had grown into a brave, adventurous person over the summer. She helped save lives, she jumped off cliffs, she was friends with a wolf, and she was a successful treasure hunter. As a completely new person, she took in her surroundings with a new perspective. She vowed to never forget the night or how she felt.

The curator finally announced the value of the gold, and it was more than they would ever need.

ABOUT THE AUTHOR

Melanie McClay

Melanie McClay has more than 10 years of writing experience through her marketing career. While she loves marketing, she craved the freedom to create and produce lengthier stories that were of her own making.

The Brave Samantha Series started with a simple idea. Melanie wanted to write a book for her nieces and nephews. She started the writing process by imagining Samantha's character and then created the first conflict—Samantha's fear of the woods. From there, the book took on a life of its own and the plot developed as more characters and conflicts were introduced.

If you'd like to contact Melanie McClay or learn about the next book in the series, please reach out to her at bravesamanthaseries@gmail.com or visit the website at bravesamantha.com.

Help this book get discovered by more readers and leave an online review!

Made in the USA
Coppell, TX
05 October 2020

39275681R10118